ONE HELL OF A MYSTERY

A Jesse Statham Mystery

ONE HELL OF A MYSTERY

A JESSE STATHAM MYSTERY

Jeannie Sutton Hogue
and
Joy Hilliard Padgett

Writers Club Press
San Jose New York Lincoln Shanghai

One Hell of a Mystery
A Jesse Statham Mystery

All Rights Reserved © 2001 by Jeannie Sutton Hogue

No part of this book may be reproduced or transmitted in any form or by any means, graphic, electronic, or mechanical, including photocopying, recording, taping, or by any information storage or retrieval system, without the permission in writing from the publisher.

Writers Club Press
an imprint of iUniverse.com, Inc.

For information address:
iUniverse.com, Inc.
5220 S 16th, Ste. 200
Lincoln, NE 68512
www.iuniverse.com

This is a work of fiction. All events, locations, institutions, themes, persons, characters and plot are completely fictional. Any resemblance to places or person, living or deceased, are the invention of the authors.

ISBN: 0-595-18857-5

Printed in the United States of America

Dedication

Jeannie Sutton Hogue-wishes to dedicate this book to my parents Geneva annd James Sutton, my husband, Johnny Hogue, and brother James R. Sutton for always being there for me. I also thank Dr. Norman Nelson for restoring my sight and making this a reality.

Joy Hilliard Padgett dedicates this book to her husband Tom, and children, Tom Jr., Candace, and Christian, who call me the "spaz" but love me anyway.

Joy Padgett is impassionate…delving into the passions of her characters…expressive, poignant, and intense…yet tempered with compassion…a rousing barb and then a sentimental tear.

Larry Johnson, Columnist

Carroll Star News

Foreword

Sometimes an author is "on the pages" as she is as a person. Jeannie is one such author. I first met her back in 1997 when she and I happened to attend a writer's meeting together. It was on of many for Jeannie. It was my first. After the meeting I was advised to give Jeannie a call because I needed help with a manuscript I 'd written, and Jeannie's name was given to me as someone who could possibly help. "Who in the hell are you? I didn't know what to say, but after a few lame attempts, we actually got a conversation going. And a pretty good one, from what I remember. One conversation led to another, and then another, and yet then another, until one day Jeannie commented to me that we had become pretty good friends. To that, she added, "How in the hell did I let that happen?"

And that's exactly what you get with Jeannie—honesty, sincerity, and an off-the-wall quality that makes each conversation with her fresh and exciting. And that's exactly what you're going to find in this, her first book. It's quirky, scary at times, shocking at others, but you'll quickly figure out after just a few pages that she's written something here that's very damn good. And then you realize that this modest, but extremely talented woman, is throwing some of this off-the-wall stuff at you as a smokescreen because she doesn't want you to realize just how good her writing is. But realize it you will, as soon as you turn the first few pages.

Ed Williams
Author of Sex, Dead Dogs and Me

Acknowledgements

Jeannie Sutton Hogue

I want to thank Sue B. Watters and Carolyn B. Buchannan for their never ending love and encouragment to making "Jesse" go to Maui and steeplechases where a chicken breast episode during a torenado turned into another book. David Muschell for always being a call away to talk me down. I also want to thank Ed Williams, Barbara Duffy, and Cheryl Blankennship. Eileen Babb for her friendship and humor.

Joy Hilliard Padgett

I want to thank West Georgia Writer for encoragement to my work on this book and others. I thank Bill Liggin (without him I would never have written), and Paul Bowdre, for many hours of listening.

List of Contributors

Songs by Tom Padgett
Cryin' Alone
Chicken Wangs

Introduction

Equestrian investigator, Jesse Statham, has several problems; one is that she uncovers a dead body at the racetrack where her most valued horse is kept. Jesse, along with Georgia Lee, her boss who is often called J.P., for just another pain, get into more than two "mental-pausal" women should.

As the killers of the horsey set try to cover their tracks, Jesse and Georgia are right behind them, or one step ahead. Combine all of this with a nymphomaniac friend, a secretary from hell, and a dog on Prozac, Jesse-distress.

Jesse hardly has the energy to crack open another hate mail fortune cookie that her Chinese cook concocts, while J.P. has the energy of a spastic teenager partying in her office after hours. Although completely opposite in many ways, the two are both highly respected equestrian authorities who share the rather peculiar nocturnal habit of simultaneously sleeping with fans to keep them cool and heating pads to keep them warm. These two Southern "pistol pals" are definitely not damsels in distress.

Chapter One

Say a prayer for me. Jesse's back. Life won't be easy.

This morning started out crappy. I had blown my nose until it was as red as the aftermath of a chemical peel. I hate this damn cold. My mood did not improve as I opened the door to see Sasha, my secretary, sitting behind her massive ebony desk with all sterling silver accessories. She smirked at me with a look that said, "I am so glad you have a cold; maybe you will die."

Sasha is my secretary—with an attitude. She thinks she should have my job as an equestrian investigator. Being a horse investigator means that I am paid a better than decent salary to look into the deaths of insured horses, and there are hundreds of them. I make a lot of money because I am not bad at what I do.

"What is it, Sasha?" I grabbed a Kleenex off her desk.

She leaned toward me her hands nearly blinding me with all the jewelry, her strawberry hair cut just below her petite jaw. "Since you look so great today, why don't you let me go to the race track for you?" Now Sasha is the kind of person you just want to slap the shit out of on a good day for simply breathing. She has a perfect figure, an appetite of a pig, and the metabolism of a three-year-old. She is also Merle Norman's poster child. She is one of the few secretaries who drive a new BMW, live in a penthouse, and shop at Saks Fifth Avenue. I'm not sure how she pulls it off on the salary I pay her, but she is a great office manager so I tolerate her.

I walked past her and snapped on the stereo.

"Must you play that horrible music?" Sasha grumbled as I moved to my desk.

While working I love to play my Heart and Annie Lennox CDs at the highest level I can without blowing out my speakers.

"My ears are stopped up. It helps me meditate and I get to irritate you with both." I truly believe that in a past life I killed Sasha and now I have to put up with her in this one. Karma can be a bitch.

"Anyway, Jesse," she drawled in her southerly way that makes my flesh crawl and I am Southern, "Mac called and said for you to get your butt out to the track ASAP. There has been an attempted poisoning."

Mac, a retired police officer, is head of security at the horseracing track and he usually doesn't call unless something serious is up.

I grabbed my black leather duffel bag and crammed in my Kleenex and cough syrup.

"Okay, I'm going now," I sneezed.

"Looking like that?"

"And what is wrong with the way I look?"

"Well, you have on jeans again, and that T-shirt."

"Why don't you try reading the shirt and it will give you a clue to my mood?" I poked my flat chest out at her face. It read, "I am out of estrogen AND I have a gun."

I stalked out to my van, which is my other home. It has all the comforts, plus it is big enough to mow people down. On a day like this, I really like that feature. When you drive a big white van, how can you not intimidate other drivers?"

It was a nice day considering the time of year. In Georgia, May gets pretty hot and muggy. My heart was palpitating from all of the Robitussin Type I cough suppressant for dogs I had swallowed, I use this medication when I'm too busy to get a prescription for the human formula.

I pulled into the race track gates. I drug all my stuff into Mac's office, knocking the hell out of my knee on the horse-headed, steel hitching post he has in the doorway.

"Mac, you could move that damn thing out of the way before someone gets killed," I admonished, limping in.

"Hey, kid, what's wrong with you? You look like hell."

I squinted at him through watery eyes. He looks better that way, not as intimidating.

Mac was good-looking in his time, still is in many ways. He's tall and dark with a smooth-as-silk way about him. His black hair hosts a hint of gray. Mac is also my godfather. (I learned from the best.)

"The queen bee said you had summoned me about one of your horses."

I plopped down in a dilapidated but comfortable chair. I could barely make out the smell of leather thanks to my stopped up nose, and I love the smell of leather. On the wall was a badge of his from the Atlanta swat team. I moaned and dug out the cough syrup and gulped it down then toasted, "Cheers! What have you found out?"

"How big a policy has Dirth Hartman got on his horse, Classy?"

I jerked my head up, "Hartman's horse is the one that was poisoned?"

"Would have been,. Dr. F.I. was here and gave Classy a charcoal tubing. Saved his life."

I flinched because charcoal tubing a horse is a very unpleasant job. You have to go up the nostril of the horse and feed a flexible tube containing watered charcoal down his throat until you get to the stomach. The charcoal flushes out the poison, but the horse sure as hell doesn't like it anymore than the one performing the procedure.

Classy is a big, beautiful standard bred sorrel with flaxen mane and tail. He's only four years old and already his studbook is booked for the next four seasons, a true champion harness racer.

"He's insured for two million. That's as high as the insurance company will go. I know Dirt's premiums are more than I would be willing to pay. Can we prove anything?"

"No, and quit calling him Dirt, the charcoal removed any evidence we might have gotten—neutralized whatever he got a hold of." Mac leaned back in his chair with lips pinched together.

"Is it possible that Classy got into some bad grain? Surely Dirt isn't stupid enough to think he could poison his most insured horse at the track and get away with it?"

Mac drawled, "If it had been the grain, the other horses would have been affected. They weren't. Form your own conclusion."

"Let's go talk to Dirt," I panted rising out of the soft leather chair.

As we walked across the pathway leading to the horses, it amazed me that I still get a thrill from looking at a horse. To me they are unlike any other animal tall and majestic. If you treat them right, you will never have a closer friend.

We made our way through the maze of concrete and wooden stalls. The more expensive ones face in, making a horseshoe around the main office. Each section of stalls comes with a tack room that holds an assortment of horse-related items the grain, vitamins, and supplements claim to make horses run faster, perform better, sort of like a very secretive witch's brew. A debate always ensues when the trainers compare them. Each section also contains a fire extinguisher mounted outside each stall ready to salute as we pass. The sully or hack, usually made of a bamboo-like wood material, is hooked up behind the horse. That's what the horses are taught to pull on the track. The racetrack is a training base for harness racing; it also houses Thoroughbreds, Arabians and a few quarter horses plus Paso Finos which are the Rolls Royce's of horses because you don't bounce, hardly know you are on a horse and Morgans which are normally black and very calm. In other words, it is a track for anyone with enough money to stable horses. The owners usually race their own horses, except for the Canadians who hire their drivers. Big money there.

Driving requires one hell of a lot of talent, is extremely dangerous, and if not done right, can be fatal since the driver controls the standard bred's mouth with the reins in back of a horse running fifty miles an hour. I'm a good horsewoman but not brave enough to attempt that.

We came upon Dirt, a real piece of work, outside Classy's stall. I know God has a sense of humor when I see Dirk. He is short, square-shaped, with no neck, dark hair, and a permanent lemon sucking expression. He jumped up when he saw us.

"Jesse, what are you doing here?"

I stuck my hand out to shake his; he hesitated a moment before finally reaching for it. I shake hands with men like Dirt because I've got a great grip, which irritates the crap out of them.

"Dirth, how's it going?" I responded quietly.

"Off your beaten track, aren't you?" He spat out the words, along with a stream of tobacco juice.

"No, and what's it to you?" I reached past Dirt's head and patted Classy's neck; he nickered softly.

"I don't see why you are making a federal case out of this; it was just colic."

"Yeah, a two million dollar case of colic." I kept smiling.

"I don't know why you assume money has anything to do with it, and I don't have to stay here and talk to you." He turned on his cowboy boots with spurs and rattled off.

Guess I should have been nicer since he has a heart problem. Nah, I thought.

I looked at Mac. "Such a warm person."

"Damn, Jesse, you practically accused him of trying to kill his horse."

"Did not."

"Yes, you did. You were never one for tact."

"I just like to cut to the chase."

"I know. Believe me, I know. How about some lunch?"

"No, thanks. I have to go find the vet and talk to him."

Mac patted me on the shoulder, "How's Georgia Lee?"

I cringed. Georgia Lee, those who know her on a professional level call her J.P. 'just a pain.' Apparently she doesn't care because even I frequently slip and call her that. She is the president of Equine Fidelity and the one person who is meaner than I am. While I enjoy physically castrating someone, she verbally castrates. We have had some heated disputes over horse policies and Sasha, whom she despises; however, I am pretty sure Mac has a crush on her. I doubt she returns the affection since she has ice water in her veins instead of blood. "She is the same goddess you worshipped last week, Mac."

Mac turned a strange shade of red. "Jesse, that's uncalled for; she is one fine woman."

I stuck a finger down my throat pretending to gag.

"I gotta go find the vet and write a report on a twelve acre farm plus the Baggetts want me to insure their latest acquisition, a new Arabian.

"All right, I'll take a rain check," Mac promised.

I managed to find Dr. F.I. in his office, which sits back from the road about half a mile and resembles a compound. F.I. has seven children and as the years have passed, he has added several buildings. The one for grooming belongs to a son. Another, a pet store, his daughter claims. A third structure is a pet portrait's building. Whenever I can, I visit because I get a kick out of watching the parade of canines and their owners in their Sunday best slicked-out-to-take-a-picture getups.

F.I. is a sweet person, the only vet who doesn't care more about money than he does animals. He also has a dark sense of humor. He tells out of town clients that I am an animal abuser, which is outrageous. Why? I don't know, but he gets a kick out of their and my reactions.

"Well, I knew you would show up sooner or later," he said when he decided to acknowledge my presence.

"Hey, Doc," I responded walking over to him.

"I guess Mac called you about Hartman's horse," he answered, walking over to the stainless steel counter crowded with drugs and syringes.

There he began filling up a bottle with a dropper as he peered at it through his half reading glasses. He looks pretty good for a country vet, brown hair and matching eyes that have seen much tragedy but would not tell you anything unless you put bamboo shoots under his fingernails to help him along.

"Yes, he did. Was it colic?"

"Jesse, you've been around horses all of your life. You damn well know almost as much about them as I do. You know colic is defined as anything to do with the stomach of a horse. Since they can't puke, it's called colic."

"I know the horse was insured."

"Seems like going to law school made you more suspicious than you should be, Jesse. You take the death or illness of every horse as personal. You have to quit doing that."

"Look who's talking," I snapped.

His phone rang and I took that as my cue to leave.

I managed to get my van turned around and headed toward my office. I had grown up on a ranch outside Atlanta near Macon. Even when I was young, I was in love with horses. I wanted to be a veterinarian, but my mother wanted me to be a nurse, so I decided, "Screw it. I'll go to law school." I never finished. I couldn't take all the junk that goes with it. Trying to be a law-abiding citizen is not prominent in my gene pool.

When I walked into the office, Sasha pounced, reminding me of a cougar.

"What happened?"

"Nothing that can be proven. Also went to the Arabian signing on the way here, great gelding. Any messages?"

"Your godson from hell called," she said, swinging her legs under her black lacquered desk. Naturally, it cost three times what mine had. Every month the beaded sterling silver frame contains the man of the moment. This month's hunk resembles Mel Gibson.

One Hell of a Mystery

"Jason?" I asked.

"Yes, and he threatened me again. I don't have to put up with that. It is not in my job description."

As I walked to my door, I muttered, "And I guess having three-hour lunches is?" and slammed the door.

The first thing I do when I come into my office is light candles, a red one for power, and a white one for calm, making my office look like an inferno. The second thing I do is put on my music; I function better when I have Annie Lennox screaming, "Would I lie to ya, honey?" especially if I have some heavy mental work to do.

In one corner of my office, I have a small fountain that is filled with rocks people have sent me over the years, some as favors, others as payment. Another corner is filled with plants in varying shades of green. I love the big Fica because I can hide behind it from Sasha if I have to.

I like my office. It's navy and rose with Queen Anne chairs and tables and terra cotta angels sitting everywhere. God knows I can use their help as much trouble as I get into. I figure the more the better. Thick plush white carpet with a huge Oriental rug ties all the colors together.

I picked up the phone to return Jason's call from the high school. While I waited for the headmaster to find him, I tried to think of which excuse he would come up with today to try to leave school. The boy is very resourceful when it comes to getting his way. He is fourteen and lives with me. His mother, a friend of mine, couldn't handle him anymore. The pressure from her divorce was too much, and she turned to drugs, then left town giving full custody to me.

Jason came on the line. "Hey, Jess, I think I'm having an aneurysm. Come get me."

"Exactly what are your symptoms, Jay?"

"I feel like my brain is going to blow a hole in my head."

"Jason, I will light a candle for you, and in a few minutes, you will be fine."

"Oh God, not the candle crap again. Why can't you be normal and just give me some Tylenol or something? Don't you care that I am near death?"

"Are you going toward the light?"

"No."

"Then go back to your class and I'll see you at home."

"I really hate you."

"The feeling is mutual," I sighed heavily and hung up.

By the time I finished my paperwork, it was time to go home. Naturally, Sasha had to have the parting comment as I left. "Georgia Lee wants to see you before you leave. Are you going home and hopefully practice makeup technique?"

"No, I thought I'd practice slashing tires on my way out," I retorted, trotting up the four flights instead of taking the elevator to the Queen of Mean's office.

J.P.'s office door is heavy leaded glass. I rapped on it and passed through a metal detector. J.P. is a nutcase about security having been stalked by a thirty-six-year-old Napoleon-type male, who had found her very sexy even though she's several years older. Go figure. Naturally, the detector screamed as I passed through. Her secretary is Tangle, a hateful thirty-one-year-old cowboy who jingles with massive silver spurs every time he takes a breath. Georgia's boy toy of the moment I figure. He is my height, thin, and always dresses in Johnny Cash black western wear. He probably has been in prison for something because his mouth never moves when he speaks and that is the way prisoners keep guards from knowing what they say. He nodded at me and flipped a switch under his desk to shut off the screaming detector. "You packing again, Statham?"

I looked at my duffel bag. "Of course I am, this is the state of Georgia. Is IT in?"

He pointed toward an even heavier leaded door.

I entered the presidential suite which makes my office look like a tar paper shack. Heavy Victorian brocade furniture is arranged so that you feel as if you have entered the Smithsonian; Georgia's own oil and watercolors grace the walls. Behind her desk is a four by six-foot watercolor that she painted of a Franklinia Alatamaha, a rare camellia-like blossom which once grew along the Alatamaha River in south Georgia. A black baby grand dominates one corner, digital, of course. Her favorite western singer croons from J.P.'s state-of-the-art stereo, "Cryin' alone, knowing you're gone, and I don't know the reason, you did me so wrong. I know now that life, as we know it is through, but I just can't take my mind off of you." I figure that after the queen gets through terrifying, she parties madly in here with her cowboy watchdog. Her desk is a very thin French thing, and if I smacked it with my hand, it would buckle like a house of cards. An expensive gold Mont Blanc pen on one side and a voodoo doll hovers on one of its corners She has several stashed in various places; I know she keeps one in her Cadillac. I saw her wreak havoc on one man who thought he could intimidate her. It was not a pretty sight to see that man groveling once she cast one of her evil spells on him.

J.P. was dressed in a celery green silk suit, with a bright clingy purple blouse, emerald earrings and diamonds glinting off her small hands and ears. She has natural blonde hair worn short and spiked.

She cleared her throat meeting my eyes. "I heard you coming in."

"Damn, and I pride myself on being half Indian."

She sorta smiled; at least, her mouth twitched which I took as a smile. I was wrong.

"Jesse, what am I going to do with you? You are the best damn investigator I have, but you keep appearing in the papers not exactly putting Equine Fidelity in the best light.

I narrowed my eyes. "At least it's free advertising."

She rolled her hazel greens. "For God's sake, Jesse, don't be flippant. Quit kicking our clients in the head or I will be forced to send you back to anger management class."

I stepped closer and peered down at her. "Tell me you're kidding."

Georgia stood up and snarled, "Not joking. Try me."

"Double shit! All I did was rescue some starving horses from an asshole that refused to feed them and…"

"Kicked the man in the head," she injected, her glare and voice glaciers. "Statham, behave." Her index finger pointed. I was dismissed.

As I turned down my long driveway, I heard a hellish noise coming from behind me. A green helicopter loomed in my rear view mirror. It scared the crap out of me. The skids were practically on top of my van. It was my neighbor Vernon, who lives down the road from me. He works for the forestry unit and gets to bring his helicopter home. He was one of the best pilots in Vietnam and you just get this feeling that he used a lot of drugs over there. He hasn't gotten over my having him arrested for shooting at my horses; therefore, he takes pleasure in chasing me around and doing sneak attacks in his helicopter. One day I am going to be waiting with my shotgun and blow Vernon's ass out of the sky.

Chapter Two

Prince and Flazon, my horses, nickered and chased my van down the driveway. Barney, my Springer Spaniel, tried to chew my tire off as I parked. As usual he barked at me as I got out. I swear he cusses at me in dog language. This time he gave me the where the hell have you been and why didn't I get to go routine.

I turned toward the house which my husband, Johnathan, and I built in the woods over fifteen years ago on thirty acres of land. The original plan for the house had eight rooms. However, Johnathan got carried away and now it is a wooden maze. I lost count of the additional rooms that Johnathn decided were essential to our daily living, and, instead of the one staircase, we actually ended up with three. I can easily find the den, kitchen, and our bedroom; however, I sometimes become disoriented when I try to find where others in our household sleep. The location was supposed to be peaceful, and was, until I went to war with all of our neighbors. I can't help it if they are upset when my horses get out and eat their flowers. As I explained to them, (I picked this tidbit up in law school) some things are acts of God.

Bone tired I dragged into the house and headed straight upstairs to the bathtub. I love a hot bubble bath. I had jets on the tub until Jason decided I didn't deserve them and dismantled them with a screwdriver to see where the water goes. Johnathan has them on his "to fix list." Meanwhile, if I get desperate enough, I put my head under the water, blow bubbles, and pretend to be in a whirlpool. Another oddity that relaxes me is a spell that I practice before bathing. I read about it in one of my spell books. I write my name in the water with my finger before getting in, then say: "Water blue, water green, please relax me and make me serene" twelve times. I tried it but lost count, said the hell with it, and got in to bathe. I lasted about ten minutes before I dragged myself out and pulled on clean clothes.

Barney and I made our way to the kitchen to see what Tommy was preparing for dinner. Tommy, twenty-three, Chinese, small and powerfully built with a martial arts black belt, is on parole for breaking and entering. He has lived with us almost three years. I met him while I was taking Tae Kwon Do. We usually have practice sessions after breakfast. I try to be careful around Tommy because he is very good—wouldn't want to piss him off. I get out some of my frustrations, and I assume he does also, since we rarely talk during these routines; we just grunt. I also do yoga but get tired of being able to kiss my own ass. When he first came to live with us, there were rumors circulating that he had been in the Chinese Triad which stands for earth, heaven, and man. These gangs are into murder, drugs, and prostitution. They earn more in one year than the total US currency now in circulation. Hong Kong has roughly three hundred thousand members, and that is just one of a couple of hundred groups worldwide. How Tommy got away from them is still a mystery -probably because the assistant district attorney was going to put him away for what I felt was a trumped up breaking and entering when the police found him outside a posh house with broken glass around him. I strongly suggested that the district attorney let Tommy stay with Johnathan and me instead of going to jail. He quickly agreed to my suggestion after I reminded him of the night I had once caught him having sex with Sasha at the office. He knew his wife would not relish that information. Tommy calls what I did blackmail; I call it fair.

He is, like Johnathan, a man of few words, and since I have known him, he has rarely smiled. Nevertheless, he is a great cook, keeps the house halfway straight, loves horses and hates Barney; the feeling is mutual.

Tommy was busy stirring a bowl full of stuff his radio turned up to a gospel station he listens to all of the time. He refuses to tell me why he prefers gospel to rock and roll, must be a cultural thing.

"What is it?" He asked, not looking up.

"Nothing," I muttered opening the refrigerator to grab a beer, Chinese naturally, from the door. Barney was spread out like a rug in the middle of the floor; I stepped around him.

"Fine."

"All right, I just can't let go of Hartman's horse getting sick today. I have this gut feeling," I admitted, taking a long swallow.

"Hmm," was his reply, as if he knew what I was talking about.

"You think I should look over his financial statements, don't you? You are so in tune to my moods that it's scary. Thanks Tommy." I blew him a kiss.

He looked at me and resumed stirring.

Jason slammed in the back door. "I barely made it through school, today, Tommy. I think I had an aneurysm and Jesse wouldn't believe me."

I smiled at him and offered, "Would you like some juice, sweetie?"

"I would rather have a Pepsi."

"No. I had rather you drink juice. I will give you a choice, juice or water."

"Yuck," he clutched at his throat and threw himself across the kitchen table.

Tommy continued to ignore us. I handed Jason the apple juice can.

"Be thankful I'm not making you drink hot tea. Come on, help me feed the horses."

I took the lead while Jason played kickball with pinecones and every stick that was on the ground. He smashed the empty apple juice can under his shoe at least ten times. We made it to a smaller version of the palace: the Barn. Its exterior is cedar; inside there are six stalls and a small, enclosed office. The roof is terra cotta. The heating bill is outrageous in the winter often soaring to six hundred dollars a month, but we all love the Barn. When we initially planned to build it, Johnathan wanted a tin roof but was outvoted. Rain on tin scares the horses. While

I was getting out the grain and measuring it, Jason was supposed to be getting the hay. For some strange reason, he was carrying it strand by strand, waiting for my reaction out of the corner of his eye.

"Jesse, do you think this is too much?" He smirked.

He had approximately twenty strands in front of the horses. They were stomping their hooves, getting really pissed off. You don't mess with horses at feeding time. They nicker when they see you coming, but you have about two seconds to put the feed out and get out of their way.

"Jason, you know that new Game Boy you have been wanting?"

"Yeah."

"Why don't we go the mall after dinner and get it?"

"Are you serious?" He started jumping up and down.

"Of course, I am, just as soon as we eat. Oh yeah, before I forget, you need to give Flazon forty thousand strands, and since Prince is bigger, you probably need to go forty-eight thousand. God, you're one smart kid to think of counting it. I am impressed. See you at the house." I turned to go.

Jason looked as if I had shot him. "It will take me all night to count that is not fair."

"Sure it is. I promise, when you are finished, we will go."

"The store will be closed by then."

"Well, you had better start counting."

As I turned to the house, my beeper started vibrating violently. I will never get used to having shock treatments on my hip when getting a phone beep. Mac's number appeared. I called him from the Barn. He answered on the first ring.

"Mac, what's up?"

"You won't believe who just bought Classy."

"Who? I didn't know he was for sale."

"Do you remember Jane Glasglow?"

"Remember her? I was in her husband's class in law school. He was a real fool, extremely hateful, but he was the nicer of the two."

"She bought Classy. Seems she wants to be in the horsy set."

"Sounds like her. She doesn't know one end of a horse from the other."

"Hartman sold him about three hours after you left."

"Then I must have made him uneasy."

"Jesse, you are so suspicious," he chuckled.

"Oh, and you're not?"

"Come by in the morning and check things out. I can't wait until you see her," he answered before I hung up.

Johnathan was standing in the living room when I walked in. In twenty years of marriage, he has never used my name. He calls me Dolls. I think that he thinks it is endearing, but sometimes I wonder if it's because he just doesn't remember my name. He is a genius at computers and mechanical things, has a wonderfully dry sense of humor, and puts up with my taking in strays—human and animal. He is the most patient, kind person I know. Sometimes he is so patient I wonder if he is alive. He is also very good looking, (although I don't tell him so) six feet tall with blonde hair and steely blue eyes. He put himself through college by playing football. I love his line backer bod.

"Hey, Dolls, your brain on overtime again?" He kissed me on the cheek.

"No, why?"

"You're looking mighty serious about something," he replied.

"There is a small thing going on at the track."

"What?"

Must all the men I live with talk my head off? I thought.

"First, there was a case of colic; Classy almost died."

Johnathan sat down in his chair that no one else can sit in because it is shaped to his body and his only and looked at me.

"You are involved. How?"

"Well, you know Hartman insured him for a great deal of money."

"And naturally, you are worried."

"Yeah. I don't seem to be able to let it go."

"You'll figure it out. I have faith in you."

I smiled at him. "You are sooo helpful."

Tommy came in the door to announce dinner.

He shouted, "Dinner" and backed out.

"Where's the boy?" Johnathan asked as we moved into the dining room.

"He came up with this wonderful way to feed the horses. He should be in a little later."

Tommy had cooked Moo Shu Pork. I forgot to mention that all he can and will cook is Chinese. As we were finishing dinner, I heard the back door slam. Jason walked in with hay all over him looking frustrated.

"I'm finished."

"Jay, go wash up and come eat."

"I heard you came up with a new way to feed the horses," Johnathan smiled.

Tommy chose to remain silent.

Jason said, "Yeah, right," and left the room.

While he was gone, I went over to the china cabinet, got out the Game Boy I had bought, and put it by his plate.

When he sat down, he noticed the wrapped gift. "What's this?"

"Open it and see," I challenged.

He ripped the paper off and yelled at the top of his lungs, "No shit!"

"Jason, do not curse."

"Sorry. I can't believe you got it for me. Guess I shouldn't have pulled that stunt at the Barn?"

"Boy, when will you learn that she is always going to outsmart you?" Johnathan jabbed.

I picked up a fortune cookie and broke it in half. It read, 'Women who drink much cough syrup go to Betty Ford Clinic.'

Tommy's real cute with the fortune cookies.

Chapter Three

When the clock went off the next morning, I threw it against the wall. I have broken so many clocks that Johnathan special ordered me one made out of some kind of NASA material. I am not a morning person. If you mess with me in the mornings, I might shoot and kill you, or at least wound you. I took a shower and went to the closet to pick out a T-shirt. I have about two hundred of them and love all. Besides being comfortable, they tell the world how I'm feeling. Today's disclosed, "Stupid People Shouldn't Breathe." My cold was not any better.

I went downstairs to the kitchen where Tommy had made Egg Fu Yong. We have to get some toaster waffles. Enough is enough," I thought. As I was sipping coffee, Jason entered with his head wrapped in gauze.

"I can't go to school today. I have a fever so high I had to wrap my head up."

"You poor thing. I bet I know what caused it."

Jason was hanging over a chair barely raising his head. "You do?"

"Yes, and it's all my fault."

"It is?"

"The news reported last night, while you were in bed, that Game Boys cause brain damage and fevers, and I gave you one. How could I be such a bitch?"

"For real?"

"Give me that game back, and I swear I'll make those people rue the day they sold it to me. You go straight to bed."

"You're messing with me again." He stood straight up by now, his gauze hanging down his back.

"Get dressed," I barked.

"I'm being held hostage. I just want to go on record as saying that." He marched out clueless about how much he reminds me of me at his age.

I kissed Barney good-bye and left.

When I got to the office, Sasha had made coffee. Because my system doesn't tolerate caffeine well, I can drink only two cups in the morning and decaf the rest of the day. Sasha switches caffeine and decaf some days to torment me so I don't know if I'm shaking from my nerves, caffeine, or low blood sugar; I've been diabetic all of my life.

Sasha was dressed to kill in a tight, black silk suit, her short skirt barely covering her behind and her tailored jacket partially exposing the dainty chain she wore. She had to be wearing her Wonder Bra since her breasts almost touched her nostrils. One look at the floor would cause instant suffocation. The VP must be coming in today. She looked at my T-shirt as if it were the worst thing she had ever seen, then turned up her surgical pert nose at my ever-present sunglasses.

"I think you make enough money to at least wear a dress shirt."

"Think about this, Sasha. If we both dressed up, people would not know who is in charge."

She liked that. She almost smiled as she reached down to smooth what there was of her skirt.

"You're right," she continued. "Just made a ten o'clock appointment with a woman named Jane Glasglow, and your, uh, strange friend Ken called and wants to have lunch with you."

"Okay, thanks. Jane is working fast. By the way, call Ken for me and tell him lunch is fine."

"You know Jane?" she asked doubtfully.

"We have met, but I doubt she remembers it."

"I have a doctor's appointment at two. I need to take a long lunch."

"Are you all right?" She looked okay.

"No. I have to go to my therapist again."

If you take the word therapist a part, you have the words "the rapist." Seems contradictory to me.

"Is something wrong?" I asked, not really wanting to know.

"Well, my friend is having an affair and it's time we, uh, she made a decision about some things."

I really didn't want to hear more, but she looked at me as if waiting for me to say something.

"Good luck."

"You know, Jesse, you could do with some therapy. You could work on your inner child."

"I will think about it." I backed to my door. "You, on the other hand, need to keep working on that inner bitch."

I moved to my bookcase and turned on my CD player, lit three candles, found my reading glasses, and turned on the computer. I had two hours to kill before my meeting with Jane. I got on the Internet and searched for horses. People love to talk about horses. Some days I run across the damnedest things, people selling or trading tack as if it were gold, which it is if you can find that right silver conch or dressage bridle which you have been coveting.

My phone rang interrupting my fun with the Internet. "Statham," I answered. It was my best friend, Crystal.

She is a terrific person. We get into a lot of strange predicaments together. She is the one I called when I kicked the guy in the head. She's always ready with bail money. She is city editor at our newspaper, and we have been friends for twenty years. I wondered where she had been hiding the last few days.

"What's up, Jess? Turn that damn music down." I reached up to my CD player and switched it off. She could piss a gnat off.

"Where have you been, Crystal? I could have been dying of pneumonia for all you care."

"I have had so much crap happening here at the paper that I haven't had a minute to myself. God, it's awful being the smartest, most talented person here," she sighed.

"It must be hell."

"It is, but back to me. We need to get together tonight. I'm the only one in charge."

"I can meet you at seven," I tried to interrupt, unsuccessfully.

"We can go to the coffee house for dinner. Damn, hold on; Shelly just came in the door. She is so damn irritating," Crystal huffed.

"What the hell is it now?" She yelled at Shelly. Crystal came back on the line, excited. "Something wonderful has happened. There's a guy who's going to jump off the roof at the Regency Hotel. Gotta go. See you tonight."

There was a knock at the door. Barney came flying in, dragging a dismayed-looking Tommy behind him.

Tommy threw the leash at me. "I refuse to stay house with killer dog."

He folded his arms and stared at me. I was impressed. That's the most I had ever heard him say at one time.

I reached down and patted Barney's neck. "What did he do this time?"

"Bit me."

"Why?"

"No reason."

"Tommy, where did he bite you?"

Tommy looked at the floor and shuffled his feet. "On the butt."

"Your butt?" I looked at Barney. He was sitting erect, sort of smiling.

"Did you try to mess with him while he was eating?"

"No."

"Exactly what was going on when you allegedly got bitten?"

"Cleaning floor, that's all."

"What were you cleaning with?"

"The broom."

"That's why he bit you. He thinks anything with a handle on it is going to hurt him. It's a wonder he didn't rip your throat out. I told you that he had been abused before I got him. The man beat him with a stick. Just leave him with me and go home and throw the damn broom out."

"How do I sweep?" He asked in disbelief.

"Do what you always do, use the vacuum."

As he turned to leave, Barney growled for the hell of it.

Sasha stalked in saying, "Don't even think of leaving me here with that beast."

"I wouldn't. I think more of him than that." In the middle of the chaos, I heard a woman clearing her throat.

"Which one of you would be Mrs. Statham?"

I looked up to see Jane Glasglow standing in the doorway.

"That would be me, Jane: I am Jesse Statham. This is my assistant, Sasha."

Sasha positively glowed. She can smell money better than a bloodhound. She almost knocked my eye out with her elbow as she grabbed Jane's hand.

"Jesse, don't be silly. I am your associate, not your assistant," Sasha glared at me.

"Oh, of course, Sasha, I get all of the asses mixed up. Dumb me." Barney was sneaking up behind Jane's butt when I yelled, "Barney! Sit!" He gave Jane a dirty look and slunk over to the desk to his pillow by the desk and lay down.

"Have a seat and I'll ask my ass to be kind enough to get us coffee. Sasha?"

Sasha looked at me and smugly emphasized, "No, I don't care for any. Thanks." I glared at her. She continued, "But I have time to get you some before my appointment." She bowed out the door, slamming it.

I went to work for Equine Fidelity six years ago. I am forty-two, six-foot-tall, and my hair color changes weekly. This week the color is chestnut with red highlights, short because I am too impatient to let it grow. I am also lean and love for people to underestimate me. I chew tobacco when I get nervous, for instance, when having a pap smear or in church.

Jane is about fifty with blonde hair that Clairol, not nature, invented. She is large framed; her body screams, "Personal trainer." The woman has hidden muscles under her Chanel suit. On her left hand, she wears a diamond that is easily four carats. She could have it classified as a weapon. Thin gold watch glistened; Givenchy shoes and matching bag shout that obviously she could give a damn about alligators. A cow wouldn't have a chance around her. After she wrestled it to the ground, she'd strip its hide off for a coat and handbag, then slap the meat on a grill.

"What can I do for you, Jane?"

She had taken a seat and smiled a condescending smile that didn't quite go to her eyes, one of those looks that affirms, "I am so much better than you."

"My husband, Mr. Glasglow, and I just recently purchased a horse by the name of Classy and, naturally, I need to have the insurance transferred to my, I mean, our name."

"Naturally," I added.

"I need you to do this as quickly as possible."

"From whom and when did you buy this horse?"

"I, I mean we, purchased him yesterday from Mr. Hartman."

"You bought a horse from Dirth Hartman?" I pulled my chair closer.

"Yes, a Mr. Hartman. Why? Is there anything wrong with the horse? We had our veterinarian check him out thoroughly, I can assure you," she responded.

"You don't have to assure me, Jane. It's the insurance company you have to assure." I beamed my condescension at her.

"Our veterinarian said the horse is in tip top shape, and, of course, his blood lines are to die for," she continued, her nose going up in a snippety way.

"I see. Seems to me I heard something about that horse yesterday," I said.

"What could you have possibly heard?" she asked leaning forward in her chair.

I leaned across my desk and lowered my voice. "Colic."

"Colic?" she responded.

"That's a stomach ache for a horse."

"Well, it couldn't have been much of a concern to the veterinarian. After all, he said Classy is in great shape."

"Exactly when did he check him?" the investigator in me wanted to know.

"This morning."

"Whom did you use?" It couldn't have been F.I., I thought.

"A Dr. Smith, comes highly recommended."

I felt my right eyebrow raising, my only give-away when I play poker. "Al Smith?" I asked.

"Yes, do you know him?"

"Oh yeah."

Al Smith. I hadn't seen him in years. I guess he must have gotten his license back. His ass had been busted ten years ago for raising pit bulls to fight to the death. A real nice guy if you are a fan of Hitler's.

The door burst open and Sasha entered with a silver tray I had never seen before with cute little cookies, a china cup, and my old mug. She swooped down like a waitress in front of Jane and presented her with the coffee and cookies.

"Here you are, Mrs. Glasglow."

She took my mug and slammed it down on my desk splashing coffee everywhere. My mug also had a saying written on it: "BITE ME." I turned it toward Sasha. Jane barely acknowledged her, so I decided to irritate Jane a little more.

"Sasha, if you are not too busy, I need you to sit in on this and help me out some." Sasha had headed toward the door and almost tripped when she digested what I had said.

"Me? I mean, of course, me. Who else would you be referring to?"

She walked back to the desk, and I motioned for her to sit down. She promptly pulled her chair almost on top of mine and put the leg down on my foot. Barney lifted his head and growled.

"Okay, where were we? Sasha asked.

"Talking about Al Smith," I said.

"Doctor Smith," Jane put in.

"Now, you're being generous, Jane."

"Pardon?" Sasha said.

"Calling him a doctor."

"I was just about to tell you about this horse's heritage," Jane inserted.

"Do go on." Sasha begged. I kicked her under the desk. I hate to hear a new horse owner with a papered horse get started. Although I didn't think it was possible, Jane's head went up even higher. I could hardly make out her eyes now. All I could see was neck. I hoped we didn't have a fire. If the sprinklers went off, she would drown.

Jane started, "He is out of an English mare. Quazanart got by Byley Turk, one of the founding stallions from Turkey. His dame is of Arabian descent." I hoped they couldn't see the glazed look in my eyes. I had been feeding Barney the cookies Sasha had brought when he broke wind. He had just made a noise so loud that Jane stopped her sermon. Sasha looked like she would die of embarrassment.

"He has a sensitive stomach, sorry," I apologized.

What in the hell could I say? My dog gets gas when he eats lamb dog biscuits. After all, Jane had just eaten some herself. I chuckled at the thought of this woman nibbling on dog biscuits that Sasha had brought out not realizing they were Barney's stash.

She managed to collect herself and continued her verbal assault. "As you probably know Standardbreds come in many colors: chestnut, black, brown, gray, bay, which is reddish with a black mane and tail."

"No!" I sarcastically answered.

"Yes, and they are the fastest horses in the world. They have been clocked going fifty miles an hour."

I was thinking, I hate shit like this. Somebody shoot me.

She continued, "Of course, the most famous race is the Ascot in England. Classy would not be in that."

"A shame," I replied, sarcasm again dripping.

"Why not?" Sasha put in.

Well, duh, I thought, but Jane jumped on it.

"Darling child, Classy is a harness racer; however, he has great potential." Right, I thought, and Barney is a poodle. I couldn't take much more.

"Let's talk insurance, Jane. Do you and your husband intend to keep the same policy amount? If you are, I need to tell you up front that our vet is going to have to examine Classy."

"But Dr. Smith just examined him," she insisted.

"That's company policy. Nothing I can do about it. How about tomorrow morning at ten?" I asked trying to terminate the interview.

"Well, I guess that will have to do." Her eyes narrowed just for a moment as she got up out of the chair.

Sasha rose quickly apologizing, "I am so sorry for the inconvenience."

They sashayed out of my office together. I shuddered. What an image the two of them made.

Chapter Four

Barney and I took off in the van to meet Ken, a very different person, for lunch. Ken is talented in most things but extremely hyper. The shrinks need to increase his Ritalin again. He has been under the care of a psychiatrist for years trying to figure out why he is so restless. He is a wonderful friend—has been ever since he was ten years old. I used to beat up people who made fun of him, still do. Ken is very tall and wears his hair in a long blonde ponytail slicked back, and his favorite coat is a long black tuxedo with tails, of course, in black. He is always dressed in leather or something that is the current fashion in Paris and stays glued to a cellular phone that hangs from his watch pocket.

No one really knows from one week to the next what Ken's occupation is. At one time, he published a magazine out of New York called Fatal, but it folded. He also, Johnathan alleges, works for the Drug Enforcement Agency.

I met Ken at the usual little Italian restaurant where he feels comfortable because everyone knows his name. I had Barney with me; the weather was too hot outside to leave him in the van, so I snapped on his leash before getting out and begged him to behave. He looked at me as if to say, "No way."

When we sauntered through the door of the restaurant, the maitre de was on us like a seagull scavenging for a midmorning snack.

"Animals are not allowed, Madam," he seemed to swell to ten feet, obviously enjoying his authority.

"Are you speaking to me?"

"Yes, I am, Madam."

I tried my usual. "I'm sorry I can't see that well. That's why I have my guide dog with me."

He did not buy this. "You can't bring that animal in here."

I began fumbling with his arm, worked my way up to his face, and stuck my fingers in his eyes.

He screamed, "What in the hell are you doing?"

"Trying to get to know you. I was taught this at the blind academy," I lied.

"If you will remove your finger from my nostril, I will show you to a table," the man finally conceded.

As he grabbed my hand to pull me in the direction of the dining room, Barney lunged.

"He doesn't like people touching me."

"Call him off!"

"I can't. I, uh, he will only calm down if you take your hands off me."

"All right, you win. This time."

Barney was face to face with him snarling, so I tugged on his leash and pulled him down. By this time Ken had heard the commotion and started toward me with his arms outstretched.

"Jess! It's fine, Maurice. She's with me. And you brought Barney. Barn, Barn. How are you, boy?"

Reluctantly, the waiter shoved a chair under me, all the while giving my clothing a pitying scrutiny. We sat down at Ken's table as Barney crawled under it to sleep.

"How are you, Ken?" I asked, checking him out for signs of twitching or evasive eye contact.

"Oh, God. You wouldn't believe the shit I have been going through. Jerry, you remember him, my lover of two months? Well, we broke up again. My dad's having a fit about the $10,000 I owe him. My magazine is doing a belly flop, and to top it off I have split ends. Does that answer your question?"

I took a sip of water. "Is this in just one day or has this been occurring over a longer period of time?

"All in one day, today. I would kill myself, but that would just make too many people happy."

"Well, then I wouldn't do it. We don't want them happy."

We ordered our food: lasagna, salad, bread, and iced tea. Maurice came by and slammed down the breadbasket.

"Ken, where have you been?"

"Oh, around." He was being vague as usual.

"Doing what?"

"Just stuff. Anyway, what's going on with you and Johnathan out at the ranch? He doing okay?"

"Yes. He's fine. I'm getting over a cold, but I'll live." Maurice brought the salads. I didn't eat mine. I had a feeling that he might have spit in mine.

"Jess, would it be all right if I come out Saturday and go riding with you? I'm stressed and would love it."

I looked up at him and raised an eyebrow, one of my many talents. Ken is not a horse person. In fact, he's terrified of them. Something was up.

"Sure, Ken, come on out."

We finally got the lasagna. Now I had Barney's attention. He belly crawled under the table to get next to me. I am slim because I am on the Barney diet. Whatever I get, he automatically gets half. As I was giving Barney a noodle under the table, Ken started twitching. He couldn't stay still very long. I knew lunch was about to be over. He was getting that far away look on his face, which means he is rapidly entering another time zone.

"Okay, Jess. It was great seeing you. See you at two on Saturday."

"Ken, you are not moving your ass any where until I finish eating."

"No, I'm not."

"Liar." I knew that look from being around him for years at poker games that our fathers made us attend. Of course, we were never allowed to speak or move through these long and agonizing sessions.

Ken would zone out in a world of his own while I watched and memorized who had played which card and what cards were remaining and who had them.

He grinned at me and motioned for the check. I knew lunch was over.

Instead of going back to the office, I decided to go to the track and see what was going on with Mac. That way I could be around horses. I am sneaky that way. I pulled the van into a space in front of his office, leashed Barney, and got out. Barney loves the track so much that he struts when he walks. He set a record yanking me into Mac's office. All the dog obedience classes out the window.

Someone was sitting in my chair when we walked in, Lt. Mike Cooper. He is in his early thirties, blonde with gray eyes, and short. We don't get along at all because I think he has a tall woman complex. I have never before met anyone who hates me just for the hell of it; I, at least, try to give people a reason to despise me. Both Mac and Cooper looked up as Barney and I entered the room.

Mac grinned at me. "Jesse, come on in, sit down. You remember Mike?"

"Oh yeah. Always a pleasure," I stiffened, sticking out my hand. I knew that if he shook hands with me, Barney would lunge at him. Evidently, he knew it too.

"Nice try, Statham." Cooper smirked. "Are you sure that dog has been vaccinated for rabies?"

"Yes, but I wasn't aware that you worked in animal control now."

"You are such a smart ass. It amazes me that you still work for that ritzy insurance company." I figured Georgia Lee would have fired you by now, her being such a lady and all."

"Ms. Lee is putty in my hands, and you know the old saying: Those who can work, work for the insurance companies. The short work for peanuts." I could feel my hackles rise.

Mac interrupted our little volley. "Jesse, what brings you out?"

"My van."

Mac let out an exasperated sigh, one I remembered from childhood. He tried to remain cool by changing the subject.

"How about a cup of coffee?"

"No thanks. I have reached my caffeine intake limit."

Cooper said, "I remember how you acted when you drank too much coffee on that stake out last winter. You shot at that man three times longer than necessary. Reloaded if I member right."

"He asked for it. I only did that because you were letting a poacher escape. Besides my trigger got stuck."

"I'll come back by when you are not so busy, Mac." Cooper stood and walked out the door.

Mac shrugged his shoulders. "I give up. You're antisocial. Can't help it, I guess."

"Only with him. Guess who was in my office this morning?"

"Who?"

I propped my feet up and figured I would toy with him a while.

"Mrs. Jane Glasglow in person."

"The lawyer's wife?"

"Yep."

Mac went on, "Actually her husband has the degree, but she's the one who runs the show. Didn't he teach at the college for a while?"

"Yes, but they let him go. Seems he was screwing around with a freshman, there were several rumors about him going around for a while. He was asked to resign, eventually."

"If I remember right, she tried to run for city counsel and lost a couple of years ago."

"Well, she does have 666 stamped under her bangs."

Mac chuckled, "You need to write a book about how to make friends."

"I am. I'm going to call it I'm Okay and You're Not."

"What did she want?"

"You know that is confidential, Mac."

"You'll tell me sooner or later."

"I know. Let's just say she wants a horse insured, and she wants things to move much faster than I'm willing to let them."

"Did she remember you?"

"She didn't act like it. I'm not sure."

Mac got up and walked over to the coffeepot and refilled his cup. He seemed preoccupied. "Lt. Cooper was telling me about a strange call last night. I didn't pay any attention to it until you came in."

I was on the edge of my seat now. "What was it?"

"Seems your new friend, Jane, according to Cooper, is to meet Al Smith at the Water Park at one o'clock tomorrow. I can't think of why they would want to meet at a place for kids."

"Maybe she's regressing; she has money. Smith just got back into town. He seems to be making connections for himself again. Why did someone call Cooper about Smith?" I wondered.

"He didn't know. That's why he came out here. He wanted to know if I knew Smith was in town again."

I was biting my lower lip, something I do when mulling over a problem.

"You know, Mac, I could go to the Water Park tomorrow and try to find out what they are doing there."

"You could, but what if they spot you?"

"I could keep Jason out of school and use him as a cover. He loves the Water Park."

"Jess, be careful. You know separately there're mean, but put them together and you have…"

"Satan," I finished for him.

Barney and I high tailed it back to the office. I had to quit messing around and get to work. Sasha looked flustered as I walked in.

"Sasha, are you all right?"

"Oh Jesse, Ronald is here."

"Who is Ronald?"

"God, you don't remember? The new vice president."

"Obviously not as well as you do. You are absolutely glowing."

Her hand shot up to smooth her hair. "We are on very good terms."

"No kidding. Well, where is your hunk now? Is he still in the building? I guess I should meet him."

Sasha crossed her arms. "You just missed him. He had to go to a very, very important meeting."

"Wow. I wish I were that important. Here I am just a lowly investigator, paying that son of bitch's salary, and yours, I might add," I continued. "Why don't you come with me tomorrow, go undercover?"

"Really!" She was excited now.

"Yes, and bring a bathing suit."

"Why will I need a bathing suit?"

"It's a secret, but if you want to go, bring a swimsuit and a big hat."

I worked on the Baggett policy doing back ground checks and matching papers for the Arabian association until it was time to meet Crystal.

I told Sasha. "Gotta go or I'll be late meeting Crystal. I'm leaving Barney here while I go eat."

It was seven on the dot when I met Crystal. As usual she was dressed to the nines. I wonder if she and Crystal were related in another life. She is medium tall, has black hair, is very brisk, and sighs all the time—loudly. She is also bitchy at times. She is the only person I have ever heard of who wears shoulder pads to bed because she thinks she looks like crap without them. She's been married five times and thinks of having sex with every man she comes into contact with. She has a record number of fantasies and has yet to have an affair. She and her husband, Frank, have been married for five years, a record.

As usual she swooped in like a hurricane. Loves to make an entrance. Being friends with her can be very trying at times.

"I'm here," she screeched, startling everyone in the room.

She sat down in the small chair the coffeehouse provides for ambiance I guess. The waiter finally acknowledged our presence and came for our order.

"I'll have a leaded cappuccino to start with and an order of buffalo wings," Crystal dismissed him.

"Whoa, wait. I'll take the coffee of the day and we can split the wings. Make mine a decaf." He wrote the order down and trotted back to his college buddies at the coffee bar. He could not have been over nineteen.

"I could have sex with him." Crystal looked hungrily at the poor boy.

"How was work?" I tried to detract her libido.

"I'm so stressed. It's unbelievable. I don't see how I do all that I do."

"Yeah, meanwhile I guess you think my job is peaches and cream."

"Anyway, Frank and I are going to add an addition to our house."

"Why? I had to leave Barney at the office. He bit Tommy on the butt, today," I continued, trying like mad to get her to hear one word I'd said.

"One of the presses at the office caught on fire and I had to put it out. No one else reacts as fast as I do. God, I really would like to screw that boy's brains out. Don't look, but I had sex with that man at the table behind you. He still wants me."

"I'm going under cover tomorrow and thinking about taking Sasha with me."

"Good. Our food is here."

As we ate, the jukebox blared, "Chicken wangs, I love 'em so. The kind they make in Buffalo. A pure delight fit for a kang. Lord how I, oh, how I them chicken wangs. Um, um, um, them good ole chicken wangs.

"God this is good, oh yes," streamed from her mouth as she sucked wings vigorously then licked each finger. Next she started on the celery. It's really unsettling to see a woman have that much affection for a stalk of celery.

"Jesse, we need to get together more often and catch up on things."

We finished our meal, paid the bill, and exited the restaurant, where Crystal pulled out a cigarette and began puffing. She had to have pulled the smoke down to her toes with the force she used. As we walked to the parking lot together, Crystal also whipped out a gold lipstick, puckered up, and smacked her redder than red lips together. We hugged each other and parted.

It was dark by this time, so I sped to the office to get Barney before I went home.

When I got off the elevator, I could hear Barney barking and growling. Someone was in my office. I dug my forty-five out of the holster with two hands and slowly hugged the wall before peering around the door. I had the hammer back and intended to blow the hell out of whatever moved. Someone knocked me on my ass as I entered. Hit me hard, and I went down grabbing at a sweater with one hand and clutching the gun with the other. A red and white blur chased after the thing, and within seconds Barney connected with a leg. I fumbled again with the sweater and the fabric stretched releasing an arm. Th intruder was trying to kick Barney. As I released the sweater, I hit him in the crotch by swinging the gun up. Damn, I'd had enough already.

He screamed and fell to the floor as I turned the lights on so I could see. I kept the gun leveled at his head and called Barney off.

"Who are you and what in the hell are you doing in my office?"

He was still bent over with his face between his legs. I picked up the phone and dialed 911.

"I have a b and e at the Providence building at 452 Peach Boulevard, office number 201. I have a gun and if he sneezes, he will meet God in about three seconds." I hung up.

The man was wiry with a small frame, and when he raised his head, I noticed a disgusting black sprout of hair on his chin.

"You and your dog almost killed me." He seemed to be recovering. Holding his crotch, he tried to get up.

"Stay down or I promise it will not be a problem to shoot you." I waved my gun at him. Barney started growling.

"I work here," he said sitting back down and looking nervous.

"Yeah right. I know everyone in this building and you just happened into my office at night? Shut up until the police get here."

We sat there in silence for about ten minutes; then he started stuttering, "I, I, I most certainly do work here. I have an office upstairs. My name is Live. Ronald Live. I am the new vice president. I will have you fired for this."

A moment later, Cooper, gun drawn, burst through the door with several policemen,

"Statham, I see you have just tried to kill your boss. I heard his part of the conversation coming in the door."

I refused to put my gun down. Instead, I turned it on Cooper.

"Well, you took your damn time getting here."

"Can I get up now or will Cujo bite me? I came into this office to get a file and that dog went ballistic and attacked me. When I tried to get out the door, this woman grabbed me and hit me in the testicles with her gun and threatened to shoot me."

Cooper was smiling at me. "Mr. Live, let me help you up," he extended his hand. When he got to his feet, he was obviously pissed.

"I promise to have your job for this." With that Mr. Ronald Live turned on his heel, stumbled, and limped out.

Cooper continued to smile. I continued to hold my gun. "Jesse, you can put your gun up now. Your burglar's gone. I can not believe you tried to shoot your boss."

"I didn't know he worked here. I have never laid eyes on him before. So shut the hell up."

"Well, you made a wonderful first impression. Come on, let's go boys before she makes a citizen's arrest on the janitor," he laughed.

"Get out of my office before my other personality emerges. The meaner one."

I patted Barney and knew that at that moment he was my only friend. We slowly made our way out of the building, and I pulled one of the large metal trashcans up to the entrance making sure Ronald would trip over it when he left.

When I got home, I practically crawled into the living room where Johnathan, Tommy and Jason were piled up in front of a blaring television. They were blissfully watching a war movie and eating popcorn.

"I'm going to take a hot bath and go to bed," I announced and climbed the stairs. I couldn't deal with anything else today.

Chapter Five

The next morning I groped my way to Jason's room and knocked on the door. He moaned for me to come in.

The room was trashed, clothes wrapped around every chair. His desk was littered with empty sacks of chips and cans of coke, and several mud-stained socks dotted what had once been white carpet. I had let him decorate after Pat, his mother, had left him. He had painted everything including the walls red. I figured he must have been going through an anger stage; however, every time I have to go in that room, my brain feels as though it has been fried. There is a giant voodoo doll on his bed with huge pins sticking out of the pubic area. I'll have to have a serious talk with him about this. Maybe we could use more therapy.

"Jason, you can't go to school today. I need you to go with me to Water Park." That really messed up his mind.

"No way," he said.

"Way. Get your bathing suit and I'll meet you downstairs for breakfast in twenty minutes."

As I entered the kitchen, I couldn't quite place the smell. I plopped down in the nearest chair and waited for Tommy to tell me what was for breakfast, but he said nothing.

"Okay, Tommy, what did you cook?"

"Noodles and eggs." Always the man of few words.

Our cholesterol level has to be high. I have to buy some frozen stuff soon, flitted through my mind. He handed me a plate.

"What's with the fortune cookie at breakfast?" I asked reaching for it.

"You not come home for dinner."

"So you saved it for me," I rejoiced opening the "wrapperless" cookie. It read, "Women who sleeps with mean dog gets fleas."

I stabbed him with a dirty look.

"I'll put Barney outside today so he will not bite you, okay?"

Jason came in with his shorts and goggles on, carrying his float and rubber shoes. The boy was ready.

Johnathan walked in and looked at my plate, kissed me on the cheek and asked, "What's with the swim wear?"

Before I could answer, Tommy tossed a box at me that had come in the mail. I stuck out my tongue at him and began ripping it open. Hot damn! It was the mini camera I had ordered to put on Barney's collar so that I could take pictures of people while pretending to rub his head. I had practiced for days following Barney on my knees and understood why he is depressed. All the poor animal sees is people's knees and crotches. I loaded the film in the camera and snapped it onto Barney's collar.

Everyone looked at me and Barney, shook their heads, and resumed conversation.

Jason beamed at Johnathan. "We're going to Water Park today. Jess said I didn't have to go to school. Can you believe it?"

"Well, son, your prayers have been answered," Johnathan smiled.

"Put Barney in the barn when you leave, Johnathan. I'm doing research today."

"Okay, honey. You must have been tired last night. You didn't move a muscle."

While I checked my blood sugar, I told him what happened the previous day as he shook his head.

I reached down and adjusted the damn insulin pump dosage. There is nothing to compare with living your life attached to an I.V. stuck in your stomach. And the shots, what a thrill I get when I pop one in my arm in a crowd of people who think I'm a junkie too impatient to wait for my next fix.

"Dolls, be more careful," he warned, as he went out the door.

One Hell of a Mystery

A few minutes later as I cranked the van, I felt Jason's float slam into the back of my head. The day had officially begun.

"We have to stop and get Sasha," I told him.

"Shit," he said.

"If you cuss again, I'll take you to school."

"All right. I'll be nice all day," he promised.

I pulled up to Sasha's apartment and she was a sight to behold. She had on a black sun cover, a giant straw hat, black sunglasses, and black sandals to match her black beach bag. I would have sworn she had designer sun lotion to go with the outfit. I figured when I took my jeans and T-shirt off and she saw my blue K-Mart mallet suit, she would stroke out. A cloud of perfume followed her into the car.

"What kind of perfume is that?" I asked as she and Jason glared at each other.

"Jason, get in the back and let Sasha sit in front."

Jason gave her a look that said, "Die" and she stared back at him with a look that echoed, "Ditto."

"It's called Black Magic."

Of course, I thought, to complete the outfit. Must you marinate in it?

Meanwhile, Jason began gnawing on his float and kicking the back of her seat. I must have been crazy to bring these two characters.

Water Park is a great place for our area. It has water slides of all sizes and a cement water lane that you can float around in all day. The lane extends under several bridges. Trucked-in ferns and palms underneath create an illusion of a jungle stream. The park is on about twenty acres. There's a McDonalds, several rows of lockers, and nice changing rooms in the compound. There are several deep pools that you can go into. Floats and inner tubes are furnished. A handsome lifeguard hands them out. We grabbed ours and rushed over to rent a locker. The place was filling with people of all ages.

Within minutes, Jason decided that he had had enough waiting around and led us to a fifty-foot slide. I looked around for Jane and didn't see her, so I fell in line for the slide.

"I'm not going on that." Sasha dug in her sandals and refused to budge.

"Come on, Sasha. It's part of the job." I coaxed.

I'm afraid of heights and I'm not going." Crystal's nervous that way.

"It's not that bad Sasha," Jason lied. "You can ride between me and Jess," he grinned wickedly.

"Sasha, if you want to make more money at work, you have to take some risks." I knew that would get her going if nothing else did.

"More money? I'll try it." We were moving along the line pretty fast. When we started to mount the steps to go up, Sasha tried to turn back, but the crowd behind blocked us.

"It will be okay. Take deep breaths," I encouraged.

"They don't make enough air for this," she wheezed, clinging to her hat as we neared the top.

The man at the top in charge of the huge rafts motioned that we were next. The raft had four slots in it. Jason grabbed Sasha's arm and between him and the man sort of plopped her into the second seat. I got in last.

The last thing I heard as we went roaring off down the spinning water slide was Sasha screaming, "Mother of God. We are going to die. Oh shit. Somebody help me. Jesse, I hate your damn guts. I quit. Shiiiiiiiiiiiiiiiiiiiiiit!"

By this time, Jason was hollering his head off and waving his arms. I was hanging on for dear life as we went round and round. There was a small pool that we were supposed to land in, but Jason had other ideas. As we neared the end of the wild ride, he started standing up and shaking the raft with his feet. I tried to grab him to make him sit down, but that made things worse. The raft flipped upside down with all three of us on the bottom. When I tried to get up, I ripped my ass on the cement.

When I finally got the water out of my eyes, I saw Jason laughing his guts out and pointing to a black soggy Sasha. Her hat was limp, one of her sandals was gone, and her sunglasses were rapidly floating away. She was pissed.

"I'm going to the ladies room, Jessica, and take a Valium. Then I'm going to lie down in a chair for awhile," she stiffly announced, marching off.

I looked accusingly at Jason. "You are grounded for the rest of your natural life, you little shit. Come on." I almost snatched his arm off as I led him out of the area to the big pool. I sat in one of the lounge chairs to wait for Sasha to reappear.

"Can I go get a Coke?" he asked.

"No," I countered.

"I'm thirsty. I need a Coke."

"What part of "no" don't you get and I will explain it to you." I was digging around in my bag trying to find the Total Eclipse lotion that is supposed to block out everything including lasers.

Jason slung himself on the chair next to mine and moaned, "Man, you are so unfair."

"Yes and I'm good at it. My mother would be so proud. Here, put some of this lotion on." I demanded handing him the bottle.

I lay back and tried to observe the crowd. I didn't want to miss Jane and Smith. Sasha appeared on my left looking better.

"If that kid pulls another stunt like that, I swear to God I'm going to the labor board." She sat down.

"Sasha, there's Jane," I whispered.

"Where? I want to say hello."

"No, fool. We are under cover. We are here to observe them."

"You mean I have to spy on wealthy people. That dog don't hunt."

"What? We have to find out who she's meeting and what they are talking about," I explained, turning to Jason who had been extremely quiet. He had made a pile of lotion on the cement and was writing his name in it with his finger.

"What are you doing, Jason?"

He lay on his stomach writing, "I'm bored."

"Well, quit and clean it up or I will have the lifeguard arrest you."

"Promises, promises." He got up and went to find paper towels, I hoped.

Smith waltzed up to Jane at the edge of the pool. He hadn't changed much—dark blonde hair, six foot, and so tanned on sunless tanning lotion that you could hardly believe that he had been in prison for several years. He had on khaki shorts that I assumed would double as a bathing suit, and he and Jane seemed quite chummy. She was looking very elegant in a one-piece navy Dior, with matching navy hat. She even wore her gold watch near water, something a klutz like me finds amazing.

They walked to a table and sat.

I hit Sasha on the arm and poked Jason. "We have to get closer to them," I said. "I need to hear what they are saying." Jane stood up and ambled over to the big pool. Smith followed her, stopping at the lifeguard to pick up two huge inner tubes.

"Come on, you guys," I barked.

"No." Sasha had a defiant look. "I can't take anymore water."

"For God's sake, Sasha. It's just the damn swimming pool. Get your ass up. You too, Jason. Let's slowly walk into the pool with our inner tubes and just float up next to them. Surely between the three of us we can hear something." They shuffled behind me like they were being led to the gas chamber.

Jason got into his inner tube and grumped, "This is so boring," and floated down the incline of the pool with his face stuck down in the water. As we floated in the water, Sasha remarked, "Maybe this won't be so bad."

Thank God, her attitude is changing a little, I thought. I was wrong.

"I better not get my hair wet again. You owe me forty bucks for the slide incident," Sasha pouted.

"Yeah, right. Let's get nearer and pray we don't float next to society's finest." There were more people getting in the pool, and it was getting crowded.

"Wonder why all those people are piling in the pool. There are plenty of other things to do," Sasha remarked, looking around.

I looked for Jason. He was pretending to be a motor boat blowing bubbles in the water, as he spun round and round. We were coming up on Smith now. He turned his head in my direction. Our eyes locked. He sat straight up in the inner tube and turned white under his tan. Jason had managed to maneuver around to the other side of Jane. I headed straight for him.

"Screw it," I said under my breath. Smith had quit grinning and was trying to turn around to Jane. I nodded at Jason. He grabbed Jane's inner tube and started paddling like crazy. He was dragging her to the deep end of the pool—such a good kid. She was screaming for him to let go. I was moving in on Smith when he saw what was happening to Jane. He took off toward her. Shit, things were not going as planned.

"Come on, Sasha," I yelled. There were so many damn people in the pool now that it was almost impossible to get through them. The deep end was where Jason had taken Jane. When I finally reached Smith, he was holding on to one side of the inner tube, pulling as Jason pulled the other side.

All of a sudden a siren screeched. Everyone started screaming. The water started churning, throwing us around like corks. With four-foot waves coming at us, I tried to get to Jason but couldn't find him. I opened my mouth to scream as water gushed down my throat: wave after wave hit hard. I finally decided to ride it out. After about five minutes the water started to calm down a little, but the force of the waves was so strong that it kept throwing me back to the shallow end. I unscrewed my body from the tube and ducked under the water to swim to the side. I finally made it and saw a bright pink neon bathing suit. I made a grab for it. It was a grinning Jason.

Together we stumbled toward the shallow end. People were still screaming and flopping around like fish. I looked up and Sasha had her butt stuck in the inner tube. Every time she tried to get up, a wave knocked her down. She looked like a drowned rat. I put my arm out to stop her inner tube from moving and helped her up. She leaned on me weeping. "I just had a near death experience. I saw all of my dead relatives," she sobbed as I led her to a chair.

"Even my grandmother." She kept saying, 'You have to go back. Your work here is not finished.'" Sasha was shaking badly now.

"You will be all right, Sasha." I was rubbing her back, looking for a damn lifeguard.

"I saw God, Jess."

"I know, Sasha."

"It changed my life. I will be nicer to people now, help the poor. I'll even be nice to Barney."

"That's good." Finally, a lifeguard walked by.

I grabbed him by the throat and demanded, "What in the hell is wrong with that damn swimming pool we were just in? This woman is in shock."

"Oh, you mean the Frantic Atlantic?" he questioned.

"I don't want to know the damn name of it. I want to know why the hell we were not warned what it did."

"I dunno know," he rubbed his chin. "We rang the siren before it started."

"Go get the manager. I want somebody's ass for this." I was furious.

"We don't have one. He quit."

Sasha had a strange expression on her face. She was looking toward the sky.

"Jess, I see angels waving at me."

"Jason, go to the van. There is a bottle of wine in the back that I brought. Smuggle it in."

"Can I have some?"

"No. Go get the wine," I hissed.

"I'm just as upset as she is." He grabbed the keys and left.

"Run like the wind," I yelled at him. That only made him go slower.

"You need to lie back in the lounge, Sasha, and try to be quiet."

"You really are concerned about me. That's sweet."

I just wanted her to shut up so I could try to find out where Smith and Jane had gone.

"Jess, I am good at being a private investigator, aren't I?"

Now she was delusional.

"Oh yes. We are a regular Cagney and Lacy. Where in the hell was Jason? I spotted the back of Jane's head in a chair seven rows ahead of us. Good.

Jason walked up with a giant bulge in front of his bathing suit.

"I'm back."

"Give me the bottle." I snatched it out of his trunks.

"You're going to make me important." He grabbed his crotch doubling over.

"Impotent, and I don't care."

As I was pouring the Chablis into a paper cup, the lifeguard appeared at my elbow.

"You can't have alcoholic beverages in here. We don't allow it."

"Go away," I snarled. "Sasha, drink this." I handed her the wine. She gulped it down without breathing. Her coloring began to improve, but she was still way too quiet.

"Jesse, you have a wonderful aura around your head, just like a rainbow."

I poured her another cup. I looked around for Jason. He had cornered a group of cute girls in bikinis and was flexing his muscles. The girls were giggling. I peered toward the front to see if Jane and Smith were still there. They were. I left the wine bottle with Sasha.

Jason was occupied with his new friends, and I decided to put Sasha's straw hat on with my big beach towel; then I sat in a chair just behind Smith.

The two were leaning close together. Jane smiled, pushing a blonde stand of wet hair behind her ear. Diamond studs dazzled in the sunlight.

Smith was saying, "We are going to have a very profitable partnership. Trust me."

"I do, hon, that's not the problem. But convincing my husband, Ben, that this is going to work is another matter."

"You can convince him. I know you can. Just remember how much we will gain for such a small investment," Smith reminded.

"When will you take care of that other matter?"

"Soon."

"Make sure that you do," Jane in insisted. "I will not tolerate any loose ends like that insurance girl. She isn't as stupid as she appears."

Thanks a lot, and Girl? I thought Who in the hell refers to me as a girl? They got up and left. I lay there under the towel and hat until I was sure they weren't coming back.

I returned to find Sasha singing "Shall We Gather at the River" at the top of her lungs. Between us Jason and I managed to get her into the van and I dropped Sasha off at her apartment and suggested that she take the rest of the day off.

When we got home, Jason dashed into the house. I had had enough of playing Sherlock and decided to brush Prince and Flazon. Barney came galloping up to greet me, then sat on his haunches and proceeded to bless me out in dog language.

I approached Prince with the halter and lead rope and put them on him. He is a quite beautiful Appaloosa, gray and black with chocolate circles. He has one blue eye and one brown. He is fifteen hands and about eleven hundred pounds and likes to act like a fool when I bring him out to brush him. I tied him to the cross ties where the electric fans run to keep the insects off. He started switching his tail back and forth. I picked up the rubber curry to loosen the dirt, going in small circles, being sure to hit all the right spots.

Finally, he started relaxing and let out that sigh I wait for that tells me he's feeling better. Then I got out my cowboy brush to move the dirt out. There is something comforting about brushing a horse. You have to do it daily, but it doesn't seem like a chore. My finishing brush with its ultra soft bristles was last. Prince gleamed like a mirror. All that was left was to clean his hooves and fly spray. He waited until the fly spray bottles came into sight before deciding to rear up and go ballistic.

"Damn, Prince. Give me a heart attack, why don't you?"

I unfastened him and led him back to the pasture gate. He whirled, snorted, tossed his head and took off at a hundred miles an hour.

While I worked on Flazon, I thought about what Jane and Smith had discussed. I still don't have a clue as to what they were up to. I gave Flazon a carrot for acting decent and turned him out to pasture.

Walking back to the house, I remembered that I needed to call Dr. F.I. and get his report on Classy for the policy. If the horse passed, I would have to write Jane one large horse policy.

I marched into the den and called F.I.

He answered on the fourth ring, "Animal Clinic, what do you want?" He was being nicer than usual. "Where is the new girl you hired, Caroline?"

"Gone to get some lunch. It has been a mad house here. I'm backed up because I had to examine Hartman's horse for you."

"What did you find out?"

"Seemed good enough on the outside, but…"

"But what?"

"Didn't seem right on the inside."

I got up off the couch. "What didn't seem right?"

"The inside," he answered.

"Will you please get to the damn point? What in the hell is wrong with the horse's insides?"

"I didn't realize you were off your kryptonite pills again," he said.

"I would appreciate it if you and Johnathan would refrain from discussing my hormone pills," I retorted angrily.

Well, are you taking them?"

"Yes, damn it, I am."

"God help us if you aren't. I'm trying to tell you there is nothing wrong with the horse I examined."

"So Hartman's horse checked out?"

"No. I said the horse I looked at checked out."

"That's what I said."

"You said Hartman's horse. The horse I saw today looked like Classy, but his stomach wasn't."

"Wasn't what?"

"Classy's."

"Stomach?"

"Right. Now you're getting it. The horse I looked at today was ready as rain to be insured."

"But you suspect it wasn't Classy?" I persisted.

"Sure as hell looked like him."

"But wasn't."

"Right."

"Well F.I., what am I supposed to do now? You tell me a horse that I'm suppose to insure for two million dollars isn't the right horse on the insides?"

"Guess you'll have to figure it out. Gotta go. I'm backed up enough."

I hung the phone up and walked around biting my lip. Barney came in and lay on his pillow. I had to call Mac and find out what was going on with the horses at the track.

Chapter Six

No. I needed to do a sneak attack. I would go to the track. I called Barney, went to the kitchen, grabbed a couple of egg rolls, and called out, "Tommy, I am leaving and I am trading Jason for Barney." He grimaced.

As I pulled onto the interstate, I noticed a black lift truck on my butt. A lift truck is one of those obnoxious trucks that are three feet higher than they need to be. I call it the small penis syndrome. Usually men who drive them require a ladder to climb up the huge tires that belong on tanks. I hate drivers who get on your ass the minute you try to get on the interstate. I basically believe that they should get the death penalty.

I decided to go even slower. The black penis slowed down; if it had to pass me, it damn well could. What is the problem? I turned the tape up of George Thorogood's "Bad to the Bone" to full blast. Barney, who was buckled into his seat, gave me a happy look. He loves his music blaring. I keep his window cracked so he can hang his tongue out as we ride. I don't let it all the way down because sometimes Barney has suicidal tendencies.

I looked in the rearview mirror again; the black truck was still there.

I changed lanes, so did it. I reached under my seat to feel if my twelve-gauge was still there. It was. I checked the glove box for my stun gun. Ditto. My overhead visor holds pepper spray and cassette player numb-chucks, which Tommy had given me one Christmas. I'm a sentimental fool. Here I am, forty-five in my bag, switchblade in my pocket, and Johnathan calls me paranoid.

I was in the left lane and the exit to the track was coming up. I swerved across four lanes to the exit. "Let them follow that," I chuckled to Barney. I pulled onto the country road that leads to the track, humming to myself. I looked back again. The monster truck was still behind me. I looked closer, but I couldn't see through the black tinted windshield. Must be going to the track.

I decided to stop at the little deserted gas station coming up. If the truck stopped, I could pretend to get out, then jump back in, and hightail it to Mac's place. I pulled the van up to the pump; the black truck followed. I pushed on the door of the van and pretended to get out.

All of a sudden, my door was jerked open and I tumbled to the ground. I struggled to get on my feet and a cowboy looking type kicked me in the stomach. I went down ripping my knees and jeans on cold gravel. Barney was barking like crazy. Someone had shut the door, so he couldn't get out. By now I realized that there were two cowboys. One of them suddenly pulled me up, grabbed my left arm, and twisted it behind my back. Hurt like hell. The other one pulled a gun out and smiled at me. In spite of the pain in my arm, I studied him closely. He was short with mean black little eyes and a mustache had to be Italian.

The tall one twisted my arm even harder. "Hey, Len, let's put her in the car and we can have some fun."

The tall one ordered, "Shut up. You know what we are supposed to do."

"Tell me what you want. I don't know," I said through clenched teeth feeling even more pain in my arm.

"Sure you do, play that game with us and you'll get hurt."

Out of the blue, the tall cowboy slapped me upside the back of my head while he pinned my arm behind me. That did it. I was going to try and find out more. No one, but no one hits me in the head.

I brought my knee up, hitting him in the teeth, and his blood spewed everywhere from his mouth. I then jammed my left elbow down into his groin. As Shorty lunged for me, I put my left foot behind his ankle and my right foot into his kneecap. I heard it snap. I yanked the van door open, unsnapped Barney's seat belt, and out he bounded—all teeth. I quickly grabbed my shotgun and jacked a round into it while screaming, "Okay, short shit, what is your damn problem?"

Neither could speak. They just moaned and groaned, so I decided to make them a little more nervous.

"My dog is just waiting for an opportunity to eat your liver." I leveled the shotgun at them and Barney just looked at me and smiled, then his attention shifted to the car coming up the road. I waved for the car to stop; it didn't. I guess the shotgun made its occupants wary.

The short one struggled to get up. "Get him, Barney." Barney lunged at him and bit into his favorite spot, the ass.

"Get him off me."

"No!" I yelled.

The tall one was squirming, holding his crotch, and blood was still coming from his mouth where I had kicked him.

"Tell me why you chased me all over the place, and I'll think about calling him off."

"We were just fooling around. We didn't mean any harm." Barney was still hanging on to the Italian one as he danced around.

"Why did you try to beat the hell out of me?" Forget it. I'll call the track. I reached for my cellular phone and dialed Mac's number. He answered on the first ring. I told him what was going on, and where I was.

Three minutes later he was there truck tires kicking up a cloud of dirt and dust. I have seen Mac mad a couple of times; it is not a pretty sight. His face was chalk white as he jumped from his truck. He never carries a gun that I know of. He doesn't seem to need one. He was rigid as he walked up to Barney and pulled him off the short one. Then he made quick sweep of me with his eyes and saw the blood on my arm and jeans. His face tightened further. Only his eyes moved. The two men looked fearful now. Hell, even I was getting nervous. I wished he would speak. I kept hold of the shotgun.

"Mac, do you want to tie those two up?" I asked hopefully. He said nothing. This was not good.

He finally spoke, "You work for Hartman, don't you?"

The short one answered, "We ain't got nothing to say to you."

I swear I saw the veins in Mac's jaw move. Mac leaned back onto the van.

"I suggest you answer my question."

"We don't know what you're talking about," Shorty continued.

"Go on, call the police," the tall one pleaded.

Mac reached into his back pocket and brought out a lead pipe, staring down the tall one.

"When I get through with you, you won't need the police. You'll need a morgue. I know who you work for. I recognize you from the track. Tell me what you want from her!"

"We were just having a little fun," the Italian looking one spat out.

"Wrong answer, buddy." Mac sprung toward the tall one the pipe raised above his head.

"Okay, okay, okay. Back off, man. Hartman wanted us to get everyone away from the track."

"Why?" Mac asked his voice as cold as a glazier.

"We weren't told why, just to make sure she never got there, honest to God. We weren't going to hurt her," Shorty whined.

"Like hell," I said. "You kicked me in the damn stomach, you asshole!"

"We are real sorry, miss," the bleeding one whimpered.

"Mac, what do you want to do with them. Call Cooper?"

"No, I'll take care of them myself. You go on to the track."

I didn't like the sound of that.

"I'll stay here and help you."

"Jesse, go on to the track. See what's going on. I'll handle this."

I knew arguing with him was not going to help. The two men looked at each other like trapped animals. I smiled at them as Barney and I got into the van. I looked at my stomach; the asshole had torn my insulin tube loose. My arm was bleeding, so I took the opportunity to take my blood sugar count from the cut—beats having to prick my finger.

Damn it was over 180, not good. I slowly let the window of the van down and could not resist saying, "It's been a real pleasure," as I drove off.

As I drove to the track, I couldn't help but think about Mac's past. He had been a Green Beret in Vietnam as well as a Ranger. He can be ruthless. I remember him telling me once that the only person he feared on earth was himself.

He had raised me since I was thirteen years old because my parents had basically given up on me. I didn't fit in. Mac knew that and took me in under his wing while he was still a patrol cop. With his somewhat gentle guidance, I went from a delinquent to a smart-ass teenager.

The track was very quiet when I pulled in. Normally a workout boy would be exercising a horse in the lunge ring. I didn't see anyone or anything in sight except a blue pickup that looked like hay had been brought in on it.

Barney and I climbed out of the van and ran toward the stalls made of thick oak planks, the best money can buy. As we entered the grooming area, Barney started running toward Classy's stall barking. He knows better than that. What is wrong with him? I wondered. I chased Barney past the office to the stall. The Dutch door was shut—unusual for this time of day; the doors are always open except at night or when a horse is sick.

Barney was throwing himself at the stall door. I reached for the latch and snatched it towards me. Classy's head popped out. I could see the whites of his eyes. There was dried sweat on him. That was strange. Why hadn't someone bathed him off after he was exercised?

I reached for the bottom of the door and eased Classy out to the walkway. As I turned, I saw Hartman lying on the floor in the fetal position in the corner where the hay net hung. There was blood trickling out the corner of his mouth. He looked very dead. Naturally, Barney had to sniff him. I ordered him to get out and leaned over Hartman to feel for a pulse. None. I looked around the stall and then ran for the office to call 911.

I paced the floor until I heard tires on the gravel. I looked out the door of the barn. It was Mac.

Cooper was behind him. "What's going on, Jess?" he asked as police cars roared up behind him.

"I don't know, Mac. First, I'm almost kidnapped, and then I get here and find Hartman dead. I really don't have a fucking clue as to what's going on around here. At this point I really don't give a damn. The body is in Classy's stall. Barney found him. Hello, Cooper. If you want to arrest Barney and me, go right ahead. I'm going home." I was tired, mad, and aggravated.

Mac said, "She's had enough. Let her go home. She can talk to you tomorrow."

I turned on my heel and stomped to the van. "Barney. Come. Now!"

As I backed up, I noticed everyone had gotten quiet and was watching me.

I pulled into my driveway, I saw Vernon's damn helicopter. It appeared out of nowhere. He was flying low. I swear I could see his teeth as he almost landed on the van again. I had had it. I took the twelve-gauge out from under the seat, took the safety off, and shot at him.

He banked left and took off toward his house. I slammed the van into reverse almost knocking Barney off of the front seat and took off toward Vernon's house. I was going to kill the son of a bitch. I was in his yard before he could land. Blandishing my shotgun I ran toward his helicopter on foot. It might be loaded with only birdshot, but I would retaliate.

He finally set the helicopter down and looked at me warily as he got out. He put his hands up.

"Jesse, I guess you're sort of pissed at me for spooking you like that."

I said nothing.

"Come on, Jesse, what are you planning to do, shoot me?" He started pass me to his house.

"Vernon, if you move, I swear I will shoot you." I had the safety off now.

"You won't shoot me. You're not as tough as you make out. And I get a kick out of scaring those mangy horses of yours. You should do Johnathan a favor and sell them for dog food." He saluted then turned his back on me. I shot him in the ass. He started screaming and looked wild-eyed.

His wife came out the back door in a dress naturally, and gasped, "What happened?"

"Well, I just shot your husband in the ass. If you want to call the police, please do. I will be glad to point out your pot plants over there in the woods."

I got back in the van. God, I felt better.

I made it back to the house still fuming, grabbed a beer, Chinese again, and decided to take the horses out. I checked my blood sugar adjusted the insulin and yelled at Jason to come down to the barn with me. I had Prince saddled up by the time he got there. I helped him saddle up Flazon.

"How was school today, kid?"

He grunted, "Same as always boring."

"I see. Jay, do you want to trail ride or to jump them?"

"Trail."

"Okay." We set out toward the woods, Prince leading. Flazon didn't like that and started crow hopping and prancing. He likes to lead. He calmed down when we began trotting down a small woodsy trail that winds behind the house. As usual Prince decided to go between two pine trees and almost knocked my kneecaps off. Jason snickered. I plow reined Prince back on course. He can be a handful but so sweet when he feels like it.

Jason had been riding since I had gotten a hold of him at the tender age of four. He decided to speak, "So Jesse, what kind of day did you have?"

"I found a dead body, almost got killed. Oh yeah, and I shot Vernon in the butt."

He grinned, "Just as long as you had fun."

I gently squeezed Prince's sides with my legs to urge him into a faster trot. We were coming up on the power lines now and could hand gallop and let both horses run wide open. Jason loved this part. He threw his body forward as I had taught him and let Flazon's natural rhythm take over. He is majestic when he runs. His Arabian tail snaps up, along with his head. Man, can he strut.

Prince, on the other hand, put his head down low when I hand galloped him. I could feel the power of his muscles in his hindquarters as he moved out. He is very muscular from all the years of jumping. We were all out of breath as we neared the end of the ride. I leaned back to give Prince the cue to slow down to a trot. He responded. Next, I pulled back on the reins and slowed to a walk. He does this on command. Boy, I had needed this ride to get out my frustrations of the day. Jason and I dismounted and slowly walked Prince and Flazon back to the barn. When we got there, Johnathan was waiting for us with a worried look on his face.

"Dolls, I didn't know where you had gotten off to." He held Prince's bridle as I dismounted.

"Vernon's wife called with a strange message. She said to tell you Vernon's gonna be sore for a few days, but for you not to call the narcs. Make any sense to you?"

"Yeah, I shot Vernon in the ass today." I unsaddled Prince and looked at my husband.

"Did you have a reason or were you just target practicing?" he asked handing the bridle back to me.

"He called the horses dog food, and I only used birdshot." I unhooked the bridle and turned Prince out.

"I see, by all means, he needed to be shot," he agreed.

"I knew you would understand," I said giving him a kiss.

Jason looked at us as if we were from another planet. We walked to the house arm in arm. Tommy had dinner ready.

He pointed to the table and screamed, "Dinner." I jumped. I was nervous today.

We had sweet and sour something and rice followed by the fortune cookie. I opened mine. It said, "He that eat the Kernel crack the nut." Maybe Tommy needs Prozac. I would look into it.

I stomped into the kitchen. "Tommy, are you trying to tell me something? Because I don't get what you're trying to say anymore. Are you still happy here?"

He continued to wipe the counter down. "Happy enough, considering dog is crazy, and you shoot neighbor in the butt."

I looked at him. "How do you know about Vernon?"

"I hear a gun go off. I knew it you."

"How?"

"I seen him chase you with helicopter. He scare people. I knew you hurt him someday."

"How do you feel about this, Tommy?"

"I feel okay; I wondered how long before you get him."

I have to admit it; I have some supportive men in my life.

"Tommy, are you worried that I may get into trouble?"

"He asked for it. I swear that you here with me."

"You never have to lie for me. I'm a big girl and can take the heat, but I appreciate your giving a damn."

I looked in on Jason and Johnathan. They were in the den playing chess. I used to play chess with my father and never could figure out how I won.

"Johnathan, I'm going upstairs. I've had a rotten day. My head was throbbing, probably all the MSG that is in Chinese food. "When you come to bed, how about giving me a massage?"

Johnathan never looked up. He was concentrating on his next move. "No problem. After this next game I'll work you over."

I headed straight to the tub and turned it wide open, pouring in lavender oil and Epsom salts. That is supposed to be good for a headache, plus I was getting sore from being kicked in the stomach. Boy, this was going to feel good.

I put on my terry-cloth bathrobe when I got out of the bathtub and picked up a bottle of lotion that was supposed to tighten my laugh lines. Ha. Ha. Maybe if I drank the shit, it would tighten up my butt and breasts too.

The phone rang, "Speak." I uttered into the mouthpiece.

"Cute, Jesse," spoke Georgia Lee. "How and why did you eliminate Dirth Hartman and why did you let two men beat you up?"

I could hear her clearing her throat. "This had better not make the front page, and, by the way, I have arranged another anger management class for you. It starts in two days." She hung up as Johnathan entered the room. He sat on the bed holding the Ben Gay.

"Come on, let's see what they did to you."

"How did you know?" I asked.

"Well, Amazon warrior Mac called and told me what happened. Why didn't you tell me? Lie on your back and I'll start on your shoulders. You can tell me what happened."

"I was followed and Bubba one and two decided to play dirty. I got into a little scuffle with them. Now J.P. has decided that I have to take another damn anger class. Like I need it."

I proceeded to tell him all about it. He looked at my bruises while holding me and assured me that everything would be all right. He would make those bastards pay. I fell asleep in his arms.

Chapter Seven

When the alarm clock woke me up, Johnathan was gone. I threw the clock against the wall as usual. The sound still did not stop. What was that God-awful noise? I went to the window. A bird on steroids was chirping his brains out in the tree next to the window. What was Tommy giving him to eat? I threw open the window and screamed, "SHUT UP." The bird stopped momentarily then started again. Unable to take the noise, I staggered back then stumbled to the shower. I don't know why I bathe before going to bed and in the morning. It's not like I get dirty sleeping.

I dressed in my shirt that announced, "I Have One Nerve Left and You Are On It."

As I dried my hair, I thought about the new doctor I'm going to about my hormones. He has put me on a hormone blocker, whatever the hell that is. When I asked the doctor about it, he was real vague. He thinks that I am pre-menopausal. I guess the pills work. I no longer have a desire to kill people for the hell of it at the grocery store or choke the shit out of small screaming children who raid the candy isle of every piece of candy. While doing so they are warned by their parents that if they don't stop, they will lose their television and stereos. Big wow! I believe that such stupid warnings will no doubt produce ten-year-old psychopaths overdosed on sugar.

I went into the kitchen and grabbed a cup of coffee. Tommy had made pancakes. Finally a normal breakfast, I was suspicious. I speared one of the pancakes. It was not like any I had ever had before. It was paper thin like a crepe. At this size I could eat about seventy-five of them and not gain an ounce.

"Tommy, what is this?"

"You want pancake; I make pancake."

"What did you make it out of?"

"Secret!" He beamed.

I leaned back in the kitchen chair. I was still sore. Tommy turned his gospel music back up to a shriek. I don't know why he likes it, but it seems to soothe him, but it is hell on my nerves.

"Jason already left for school?"

Tommy stretched and said, "Yes. Me and you practice Tae Kwon Do before you leave?"

I sucked more coffee." You know, Tommy, I don't think I have the time today and I am a little sore.

Tommy smirked at me, "You too soft. Maybe Ms. Lee class help you."

"You listened in on MY CALL!"

He kept smiling as I shoved the chair back and stormed out to the patio where Tommy and I practice. He joined me bowing. I bowed back stiffly. The little creep, I thought. I felt like tearing his throat out.

He kicked at me and I blocked; we spared like this a few minutes.

"You kick man in head; my aim would have hurt him more."

I was sweating a little now from halfhearted sidekicks.

"I doubt it, Tommy, you sneak. I can't believe you listened to my phone call."

He screamed "YAAAAEEEEE," jumped up, and swung his leg over my head. "I in the know around here."

"Quit screaming like that; my nerves are shot," I jabbed and stepped into him taking him by the throat surprising him.

"I am going to work now and my fortune cookie tonight had better not contain a damn death threat."

I went to the kitchen, snatched up my duffel bag, and called Barney.

Barney and I tooled down the street to my office. I recognized Cooper's car in my parking spot. That bastard. I leashed Barney and went into the building. Cooper was leaning over Sasha's desk in deep conversation. Sasha was smiling at him through those 800-watt teeth.

She must go through a gallon of Pearl White a day. I marched past them to the door of my office.

Cooper looked up and followed me in. "Do not hold my calls, Sasha; put them all through. Cooper, what is it?"

"I let you blow off your steam yesterday and didn't get a statement. Now I want you to talk to me."

I went over to the coffee that Sasha makes every morning.

"Want some?" I asked.

"Yeah."

I went to my desk. Barney had already parked on his pillow.

"Get it then."

"You are such a wonderful hostess." He poured himself a cup and sat across from me.

"I know. I got to the track; no one was around. I went in and found Dirth dead, called you, then went home. Any other questions?"

"Go over it in more detail, Statham."

"After these two fools beat the crap out of me at the old gas station, I called Mac. He took care of them. Then I went to the track to wait for him. Barney went crazy and went to Classy's stall, raising hell. Classy was in the stall all wild eyed. Oh yeah, the stall door was completely closed. Seemed odd to me."

"What?" he asked. "The door?"

"Yeah. They don't close the stall doors unless a horse is sick or at night."

"What else happened?" He was not giving up easily.

"Well I had to pee, and so did Barney."

"Very funny. I'm not interested in your bladder functions." He glared at Barney. "Or your dog's. Get back to what happened."

I wished the damn phone would ring. "I turned Classy out and checked Dirth's pulse. He was dead."

"What did you see?" He questioned further.

"I would definitely say he was having an out of body experience."

"Damn it. What did you see?"

"There was blood coming out of his mouth. Damn, don't you have a coroner to tell you this stuff?"

"Yes, did you see anything else?"

"I went to the office and dialed 911. Then you came and I left."

"That's it?' He was glaring at me as though he didn't believe me.

"Yes. Can I get to work now?"

"Heard about your undercover work at kiddy-land. I wish I could have seen you in action."

That damn Sasha. "Oh Cooper, one more thing."

He had his hand on the door. "Yeah?"

"Sasha wants to have your love child."

Reluctantly, Cooper backed out as the phone rang. I snatched it up and barked, "What?" It was Jane. Boy, was I batting a thousand today.

"Hello, this is Jane Glasglow. I need to talk to you about Classy's insurance policy."

"Why?" I demanded.

"I'm sure you heard about Dirth's untimely demise."

"Dead as a door nail is more like it."

"Yes, well whatever you wish to call it, I still own the horse," she paused.

I answered with "Well, seeing Dirth is dead, you have to deal with his wife, Anna, now."

I bet she hadn't thought about that. I was giddy with power.

"His wife?"

"Yes ma'am, haven't you met her? I assumed you had, since she owns the horse now."

"I own the damn horse now. He sold him to me in good faith." She yelled. Good! I had hit a nerve.

"No, you don't. Seems the sale isn't legal because Dirth died within the forty-eight hour period. That means you don't own it unless his wife sells him to you."

"Says who?" she snapped.

"Georgia Law!"

"I am married to a lawyer. Don't tell me about the law."

"Oh yeah. Then why don't you ask your legal eagle husband about it?"

"I would know if there were such a law. I run his office!" She was practically screaming by now.

"Well, maybe it slipped past you. I just thought his practice was basically a collection agency, going after people he can intimidate." I couldn't resist that one.

"I resent that! I will call you back after I talk to your supervisor." She slammed down the phone. Shit, why did I let her get under my skin? There was something strange about Mrs. Glasgow. Call it a feeling. I reached down for Barney and rubbed him. He moaned with pleasure. "Sasha, I'm going to the newspaper and see Crystal. I need to get out of this office for awhile. Be back later."

Minutes later, Barney and I stalked through the lobby of the newspaper office. Betsy was at her post at the receptionist desk. She is a short little woman, over forty, looks eighty, with her helmet hair lacquered. If a tornado came through and destroyed everything else, that hair would survive. Sometimes I wonder if hair spray has leaked into her brain. She is not a very nice person. She peered down her nose at me through her reading glasses and waved me into Crystal's office. The old bitch isn't real fond of Crystal either.

Crystal was on two phones at the same time, her reading glasses pushed to the top of her head. She was barking orders into the phone and nodding at me to sit down. Her fax machine was going crazy in the corner. She was dressed to the hilt in a beautiful gray business suit with matching shoes and jewelry. Of course, her makeup was perfect, too. She slammed both phones down at the same time and asked, "What's wrong?"

"Why does something have to be wrong for me to come and see my best friend?" I asked innocently.

"Because you never come by, unless something is wrong with you," she retorted, leaning back and taking a long swallow of coffee.

"I had a rotten day yesterday and a rotten morning today so far—just needed to see a friendly face."

"Well, considering who you work with and your other mentally challenged friends, I can understand your needing someone sane. I know you have to be upset if you brought Barney with you. You know how I feel about him. I hope to God my boss doesn't walk in."

Crystal squinted at me and said, "I heard that you were the one who found Hartman's body. But what has one thing got to do with the other?"

"Glasglow bought Hartman's horse."

"Oh, so you find the body and Jane calls. What did she want?"

"I'm really not sure about that. She said she wanted to insure Classy, but I have a feeling she was trying to find out about Hartman's death. I don't trust her. When I leave here, I'm going to pay my respects to the widow."

"You don't trust anybody. You don't even trust your mailman."

I stuck my tongue out at her.

"See what you can find out about the Glasglows for me, will you?" I reached out to grab Barney's leash, but was too late. He had bee-lined it over to Crystal's prized ficus in the corner and hoisted his leg to relieve himself.

Crystal went ballistic. "Get that damn dog out of here. If my tree dies, I swear I'll kill him."

"Yeah, I know. It's not like he did it on purpose. By the way some people are coming out tomorrow. Want to come?"

"Who and for what?"

"Ken and maybe a barbecue. Try to come."

One Hell of a Mystery

"All right. I think Frank is going to the car race anyway. I didn't know Tommy could do barbecue."

"He doesn't; I thought maybe I'd do it. Come on Barney!" I pulled on his leash as he tried to have sex with the leg of Crystal's desk. She turned a strange shade of white.

I started laughing, "Crystal, you know he learned all about sex from you. That is a compliment in dog language."

She picked up her three-gallon coffee cup to hurl at us as we retreated out the door.

Then I drove out to pay my respects to Anna, Hartman's wife. I turned down the long paved driveway to their house, amazed that someone could keep a yard this neat. Beautiful Cherry trees line the long driveway. In front of the white-columned mansion is a huge fountain with a gargoyle spewing water from his mouth. The place is beautiful. To the right of the mansion there are stalls that look better than my house. There are newborn foals playing in the bright green pastures—white fences surrounding them. The Hartmans had managed to buy a lot of property from Drake College.

That was a coup in itself. The college is one that you can pay your way through if you want to work with livestock. In addition, they raise horses, sheep, and cattle. They have one of the best equestrian centers in the country.

Amazing how such a slimy person like Dirth could own all this. Had owned it.

I left Barney in the van this time and cracked the windows a bit.

I knocked on the huge door. I figured no one had heard the knock even though I knocked hard enough to skin my knuckles on it. The damn door was thick. I hit the doorbell, which returned a Rebel yell. I must have jumped three feet when it did. It scared the crap out of me. Barney began barking.

The door finally opened. It was Anna. She was very thin and had dark circles under her eyes. Her long brown hair was lanky. I wondered how long she had been like this?

"Hi, Anna. I'm sorry about Dirth. May I come in?"

She had on a dress. She always did. I couldn't figure that out either.

She opened the door wider. " How sweet of you, Jesse, please do."

I cringed. I hated to be called sweet. If she told anyone about my being nice, it could ruin my reputation. She led me down the long hall toward the living room. I could hear the footsteps on the hardwood floor. Naturally, she wore dressy shoes with small heels. My white Reeboks needed replacing .She sat down on the Victorian Sofa and I sat next to her. I glanced around the room and noticed a big cherry curio cabinet full of crystal balls and crystals. Unusual, I thought. I glanced over at the fireplace and was startled to see a life-size portrait of Dirt.

"Would you have some tea with me?" she asked.

"Sure, Anna, that would be great."

She poured the tea into little cups that she just happened to have out. Then she picked up a porcelain tray of tiny cookies with yellow stuff spread all over them. I accepted the tea and food.

"If I had known you were coming, I would have made some finger sandwiches."

Does the woman ever sleep?

"Anna, what is this yellow stuff?"

"Lemon jam, of course."

"Of course," I whispered under my breath.

"Dirth was so fond of you, Jesse."

I almost choked. I put the tea down on the butler table in front of me. "He was?"

"Yes, he always talked about you. If I could have been more outspoken, maybe…" she trailed off, her eyes misty. I tried to change the subject.

"Are you still planning on selling Classy to Jane Glasglow?"

A small smile played at the corner of her mouth. Mood swing. She lowered her head, hair covering her face; "I'm not sure what to do now. I need some time to think about it."

"Then you know the sale was void when Dirt, uh Dirth passed away?" I hate that term. It's as though Dirt had actually passed a test.

"Yes. I just found that out about it this morning. His lawyer stopped by and told me."

"So I guess that means you're going to return Jane's money to her?" I asked.

"Like I said, I'm not sure what I intend to do yet. More tea?" She picked up the teapot.

"No, thanks. Have they determined what Dirth died from?" Real discreet, Jesse, I thought. I tried for a good recover. "When is the funeral?"

"Oh, there isn't going to be a funeral. I'm having a cremation, a small memorial afterwards. Are you going to attend?"

"Of course, Anna. I am throwing a small get together tomorrow. I wish you and the boys would come." I noticed that she kept rubbing her neck. She also hadn't answered my question. I had heard Dirt got his kicks by beating the hell out of her.

I could see a faint yellow bruise under her collar when she put her hand on her neck. Why she hadn't divorced him was beyond me. He had started a paint company, painting boxcars—had made enough money to buy a softball team and keep them on payroll. If she had divorced the prick, she could have easily gotten half. Then came the horses. He didn't even know how to ride. That was her thing. Before she married him, she used to show hunters and do three-day events, which required a lot of stamina. Since she had married, she hadn't done any showing that I had heard about. She and Dirth had had two sons. Both were teenagers Jeffery Dirth and Dirth Zachary. Both attended the same school as Jason.

I got up and went toward the door. When I opened it, there was a Rottweiler growling at me. Anna stepped in front of me.

"That's enough, Caesar. Sorry, Jesse."

"No problem, when did you get him?"

"About six months ago, he's very sweet."

I looked at the van. Barney had his face pushed up against the window with his nostrils flared, raising hell.

"I'll see you tomorrow, Anna. If you need anything, give me a call."

I got to the van and had to use my butt and shoulder to push Barney over. There was dog spit all over the window making it almost impossible to see through it.

"Thanks, Barney. Now shut the hell up."

His barking had pierced my eardrums. He continued to bark long after Caesar was out of sight. He finally lay down and did a couple of deep growls just for the effect. The car phone rang. It was Jason.

"Jesse, can Kevin spend the night with me?"

"When?"

"Tonight. It's Friday and I don't have school tomorrow. Please? Can he? If you just say yes, my life will be better."

"Then by all means, yes. You know how concerned I am about your having a good life."

"What's wrong with you?"

"Nothing. Make sure you check with Kevin's mother. And I want her phone number to double check that it's okay with her."

"All right. Can we ride the horses and make popcorn?"

"We'll see. I have to go now, kid. I'm almost at the track. See you tonight."

Mac didn't even look up as Barney and I walked in. I flopped down in my usual spot.

"What's going on, Mac?" I asked.

"About what?" He was going to be pissy today.

"I know you're mad about my leaving yesterday, but I couldn't handle anymore."

"So you just call me when people are beating you up, leave me here with a dead body, then come in all smiles but only when you're ready to talk."

"Screw you, Mac; I wasn't responsible for Hartman getting killed at your precious track. That's your stuff. You handle it!"

"You could have at least helped me with Cooper and Anna and Jane Glasglow; they all came out of the woodwork, when you left." He leaned back in his chair, and put his hands behind his neck. That reminded me of Anna.

"What did Anna do when she found out Dirth was dead?" I asked.

"Love your apology. She didn't do anything. Jane was on her like glue and then they got into a heated discussion about the horse. Smith came up and then they really got into it."

"About Classy?"

"Yes, about Classy. Anna decided she was going to take him out to her ranch instead of keeping him out here. Jane went off like a missile, insisting he was her horse and that Anna couldn't move him."

"Wait a minute. I talked to Jane this morning. She told me that she knew nothing about her not owning Classy. I also talked to Anna who said the same. Why are they lying?"

"Maybe they don't like you," Mac smirked.

"Cute. They had to know I would talk to you and find out what happened out here yesterday. Something's going on."

"You think? Someone hires two men to go after you. Then you decide something is going on."

"Mac, quit being such a smart ass. Tell me what Smith was doing out here."

"All I know is that he and Jane were very tight."

"Where was her husband during all of this? He never seems to be around."

"I wondered when you were going to get to that. Your thinking has slowed down a bit, Jesse. Seems Mr. Glasgow isn't around much anywhere."

I was in deep thought. " I think I'll invite them to the house tomorrow for the barbecue. You, too."

"I'm glad that you thought of me. What time?" he asked.

"Come about noon. Can you bring a couple of horses for a trail ride?"

"I take it that Tommy won't be cooking then."

"Real funny. Has F.I. been out lately?"

"No. Are you going to invite him too?"

"I was thinking maybe I could stop in tonight and talk to him."

Mac advised, "Jesse, why don't you just phone him?"

"Because I like to look at people's reactions when I talk to them in person. A phone can hide a lot."

"All right. I'll be there tomorrow."

Chapter Eight

When I got back to the office, Sasha was upset.

"Mr. Live has been looking for you all day. Where have you been? How am I supposed to run this office if I don't know where you are half the time?"

"I see your religious experience is wearing off. I'm here now. What does Mr. Live want with me?"

"He is still pretty mad about your almost having him arrested and Barney biting him." She gave Barney a dirty look.

"I would think that my hitting him in the balls with my gun would have ranked up there with Barney biting.

"Where is he now?"

"In his office. He said for you to call him the minute you got back. Evidently it must be something important."

I called upstairs and Mr. Live's secretary put me on hold. I had my pen in my hand and started doodling on a piece of paper while I waited for Mohammed to come down from his mountain. I wrote Ronald Live. Then I wrote it backwards; it spelled Evil. It fit I thought. He finally came on the line.

"Well, Mrs. Statham, I have heard from Mrs. Glasglow that you demolished her horse's insurance policy."

"Exactly how did I do that, Mr. Evil, er, I mean Mr. Live?"

"You are a very incompetent young woman, I think you have been having entirely too much free reign here, and I intend to put a stop to it."

"I feel so blessed. Do you intend to tell me how the policy is, as you put it so delicately, screwed up?" I demanded through clenched teeth.

"Don't be smart with me, young woman. Mrs. Glasglow has threatened to go to another agency if we don't clear this matter up."

"The name is Jesse, not young woman! Oh yeah, how are the testicles today? Planning any late night visits to my office? If you are, call first." He hung up on me.

I phoned Jane next. The hired help answered, but Jane managed to get on the line in about forty seconds.

"This is Mrs. Glasglow speaking."

No kidding. I was impressed. The maid was probably holding the phone up for her.

"This is Jesse Statham; I would like to invite you and your husband to a little barbecue tomorrow."

"It's very short notice," she argued.

"I am sorry for that. My secretary was supposed to mail out the invitations a week ago and she failed to do it. I wish you would come." Sucking up was getting easier for me.

"I suppose we could stop by for awhile."

I gave her directions to my house, thanked her, and hung up. I was exhausted. I looked up. Sasha was standing at the door, arms folded across her chest, glaring at me.

"I heard that. You never gave me invitations to mail anything. Why was I not invited to the big party?"

"I know, Sasha, but I had to use you as a reason for the late invite and you know you are welcome to come."

"Well, okay then. What kind of party is it?"

"Barbecue. And no, Tommy isn't cooking."

I left early so that I could stop by the grocery store to buy food for the upcoming event. I picked up steaks, ribs, hamburgers, salad stuff, and devil's food cake for dessert. I even remembered the waffles. The grocery boy who put my groceries in the van started talking. I didn't know him; he looked about seventeen with pimples on his face, and ears that stuck out. Sort of cute. All I said was "How's life treating you?"

He never slowed down from stacking in the bags. Barney had his head hanging over the back seat, looking comatose.

"My father kicked my mother in the stomach during her third trimester."

I wasn't sure what that meant, so I just shook my head sadly. By this time he was slamming the bags.

"She was pregnant with me. If my brothers don't start helping me, I'm going to blow them away." He reached for the bag with my waffles in it.

"Help you do what?" I asked.

"I'm working two jobs now. Then I have to go help my mother with her store."

"What kind of store?" I had picked up the bag with the cake in it so he couldn't smash it.

"A bread and gas store. Can you believe my father offered me a thousand dollars to forgive him?"

"No way!" I answered pretending shock.

"Way. He ran out on my mother after he kicked her; now my brothers just take money from my mom. I swear, I'm going to kill every damn one of them."

I was getting worried now. "Do you have a girlfriend?" I asked hopefully.

"Can't afford one. No time, no money."

"If you dated one with a job, it wouldn't be so expensive."

"I hadn't thought of that," he replied.

"Have you thought about therapy?"

"My mother says that I am perfectly fine. My teachers tried to get me to go, though."

"What's your mother's name?"

"Doris Smith."

"Your father is insane. What does he do?"

He slung in another bag and blurted, "He's a vet."

"A veteran of what?"

"No mam, a veterinarian," he corrected.

I felt my stomach knot. "Not Al Smith." He never slowed down from the package toss. "The one and only son of a bitch."

"I see. I hope things get better for you and your mother soon." He slammed the doors of the van. I handed him five dollars.

"That's interesting," I told Barney and drove quietly home.

I peeked into the kitchen to see if Tommy was there. How was I going to tell him about the barbecue? He was standing in the front of the stove oiling his wok. Gospel music was blaring from his small green radio on the counter. I cleared my throat. Tommy looked at me, but said nothing.

"Tommy, I need to talk to you about something."

"What?"

"Well, it seems I invited some people over tomorrow for a cook out."

"No problem. I'll just make some more sweet and sour," he proclaimed happily.

"Tommy, I have groceries melting in the van. We are having a barbecue."

He stopped smiling and stared at me accusingly. "You go to store?"

"Yes, I actually bought food. How about helping me bring it in?"

"No." He looked hurt.

"Why not?"

"You betray me!" he stormed.

"I did not. It's my house, my food, and my friends are coming over. If I want to cook for them, I can. Understand?"

"One problem." he smirked.

"What, damn it, what?" I yelled.

"You can't cook." He started laughing.

"What is so funny?" I was getting pissed.

"I help you with food tomorrow; I forgive you."

Great. He forgives me. "I need help with the groceries now!"

He followed me to the van, slapping his leg as he laughed. I was so glad to see him happy. He unloaded all the stuff and asked, "How much you pay?"

I hedged around, "Oh, about $300 or so." That just made him laugh harder. I wondered if he was on a new drug I didn't know about. We finally got the food put up, and I went to find Johnathan. I was exhausted. I heard hammering coming from the barn.

"What are you working on, Johnathan?"

"Flazon kicked a board loose last night; he must have been feeling frisky."

"Is he hurt?" I was on instant alert.

"No, Jess, everything is fine. What's on your mind?" He was sizing up the next board.

"I invited a shit load of people over for a cook out tomorrow and I just told Tommy about it."

"Oh Lord."

"Actually, he took it pretty good. He hasn't stopped laughing since I told him."

"That is not a good sign. Are you sure you explained it to him?"

"Yes, I did." I was getting defensive. I mean okay, I am not a very good cook and I am dangerous around appliances, but I could use a break.

"So who's coming?"

"Just Crystal, Jane Glasgow, her husband and, oh yeah, Ken."

"Sounds like a strange bunch. No wonder Tommy is laughing." he smiled.

"Oh shut up. It will work out fine."

"Is Mac coming?" Johnathan asked.

"Yeah, I forgot about him."

"It will be fine, honey; don't worry about it."

God, he is so calm. I wonder if his parents gave him a tranquilizer at birth. But, on the other hand, no one else could put up with all my crap like he does.

"Where is Jason?"

"He is with the kid you said could come over and stay the night."

"Kevin? Oh no, I forgot about him. I think I must be losing my mind."

"No you're not. You just got a lot going on right now."

"I had better go find Jason. See you at dinner." I gave him a kiss on the cheek.

I decided to check out the back yard to see if it was ready for company. I saw a black blur go across the back. What on earth was that? It was gone. I blinked a couple of times to make sure I wasn't imagining things. I walked past the swimming pool to the picnic tables. Everything looked pretty good. I needed to go marinate the meat and turned to the back door. Then I noticed two round black marks on the cement. Where in the hell are the grills? I am going to kill Tommy or Jason. Damn. I'll just kill both of them. If I have to go to jail for murder, I might as well make it worth my while. I walked into the kitchen.

"Where are the grills, Tommy?" I asked softly.

"They rusty, I give to Goodwill."

"No hell, they weren't. Go get them back and I mean it."

"No take backs, make me lose face." He folded his arms in front of him defensively.

I glared at him. "You are going to lose more than your damn face if you don't get those grills back. I'm not kidding you, Tommy!"

I stormed upstairs. Barney followed. I had a feeling I had lost control of my home a long time ago and it would not be easy to get back. But one of us was going to die trying. I turned on some music. Thank God, Johnathan never complains about a CD player in every room.

I needed a drink. I went to the small fridge in my bedroom, and got out the first bottle of wine that I saw. Damn, it had a cork in it. I picked the corkscrew up and stabbed it into the cork. It wasn't budging. I sat on the edge of the bed so I could get a better grip, put it between my legs and pulled; it didn't budge. I lay back on the bed and wrapped my feet around the bottle. I was straining at the cork when Jason and Kevin appeared in the doorway. Sweat was pouring off of me by now. Damn hot flashes.

Jason just shook his head and reported, "I tried to tell the counselors at school that she was an alcoholic. But they won't listen."

I sat up. "Cute, Jason. Hello, Kevin. What have you been up to?" I spied Johnathan's knife on the bureau. As I hacked away at the cork, the two boys watched me, fascinated.

"We helped Tommy take the grills to the garage."

That did it. I whacked at the cork and it fell into the bottle. I tried to regain my composure and reached for a wineglass. As I poured, I noticed I had chipped up cork floating in the glass.

"In Hawaii they consider it good manners to leave the cork in," I lied.

"No kidding?"

"She's always saying stuff like that," Jason answered.

"Right. And if you don't chew up the cork and swallow it, they eat you."

"Come on, let's go before she gets any weirder."

I was on my third glass when the phone rang. "Hell Home!" I answered.

It was Crystal. "That bad, huh?"

"I have lost control of my home and am being held hostage by a crazy little son-of-a-bitch Chinese guy who talked my godson into kidnapping my grills. Other than that, I am fine."

"What are you doing? You sound funny."

"Sucking on a piece of cork."

"Do you need any help tonight getting ready for the party?"

"No. I have everything under control."

"Yeah, it sure sounds like it. Do you have Rod Stewart playing in the background?" she continued.

"Yes, I'm trying to outplay Tommy's gospel. So far it has been a war of the speakers."

"He is pissed, isn't he?"

She is so insightful.

"Yes, but I will cook tomorrow—come hell or high water."

"See you tomorrow then." Seemed to me like she couldn't wait to hang up.

I looked at Barney. "I will a buy you a big bone if you'll go down and bite Tommy in the butt for me." He just sighed and rolled over.

I was feeling a little better. I could get used to this feeling. I had to go eat dinner and sober up some. I made Barney go with me to the dining room. He didn't want to. Everyone was sitting at the table. Tommy had turned his radio up even higher.

I could hear Jimmy Swagart saying, " I am only human!" All that man did was apologize. Tommy had made green pepper steak, Johnathan's favorite. So the little bastard wanted to play dirty, did he? Tommy smiled at me.

I stumbled to the den and turned all the speakers wide open to "Maggie May," Rod Stewart's first hit and sat down.

Johnathan ignored us as he savored the food. Traitor. Jason and Kevin just sat and watched us. I think they knew they were out of their league now. This was war. I refused to eat.

The boys were quiet. "Can we be excused?"

Was this Jason speaking?

"Sure," I answered coldly.

Tommy plunked a fortunn cookie down in front of me. Screw it. I picked it up and cracked it open. It read, "Though the fox runs, the chicken has wings." I rolled my eyes at Johnathan. I took great joy in feeding that little saying to Barney. Tommy looked at me.

"You not eat dinner," he accused me.

"No kidding! I'm not hungry."

"You not get any nicer until you eat."

"I would rather starve."

"Fine, I know not why I knock myself out when you bring dead cow home."

One Hell of a Mystery

Damn, I forgot to marinate the meat in my special prepackaged marinade.

"Tommy, I need you to come out of the kitchen for awhile. There is something that I need to do." He acted like he didn't hear me.

I got up and went to the kitchen. He followed. I grabbed the ribs, threw them into a big stainless steel pot, and poured the sauce over. I ignored him. He turned the music higher.

I went to the CD player in the corner and pushed play. Melissa Ethridge came on with "I'm the Only One." He started chanting in Buddhist. I started singing as loud as I could. Barney started howling. I picked up two pie plate tambourines and sang more. Tommy threw a dishrag at me. I picked up the pot of ribs and dumped them on his head. He turned just in time to miss the sauce.

I temporarily forgot he knew Tia Kwon Do. The little shit could really move. The ribs went all over the table and floor. Barney was delighted. Tommy looked at me like he couldn't believe I had done that. Actually, I couldn't believe it either. He stood on one foot and started to make a humming noise at the back of his throat. He put his hands together. I stood on one of my feet and started humming too. He snatched the bottle of marinade up and tried to run to the garbage disposal with it. I struck out and blocked him. He tried to kick at me. I moved to the side. He kicked the radio. That really pissed him off. Jimmy Swagart was still squawking. All I could find was a colander. I grabbed it and threw it at his head. He came at me again this time wearing the colander as a headdress.

I blocked again. "Tommy, I can make sure you don't have children if you don't stop."

Barney began to bark. Jonathan came through the door and looked at us, marinade all over me, and Tommy with a colander on his head. Barney sat there with a slab of ribs in his mouth.

"Knock it off!" Johnathan thundered. "You are supposed to be adults!"

Johnathan never loses his temper. He looked like he couldn't believe what he was seeing.

"Tommy, you go to the back. Jesse, you go upstairs!"

Tommy and I glared at each other—neither willing to back down.

Chapter Nine

Johnathan grabbed me behind the legs and threw me over his shoulder. I went straight as a board but managed to duck when we went through the doorway. After toting me upstairs, the Bod dropped me into my rattan chair in the bedroom.

"Are you going to calm down tonight?" he panted.

"I am calm."

"Jesse, you knew when you started this, he wasn't going to accept you trying to cook."

"Yeah, but I gave him a home when no one else would. I believed in him," I sulked.

"Yes, and he cares for you. But you are stepping into his territory now."

"He tried to kick me." I was still upset.

"I believe if Tommy wanted to kick you, he would have. He is a Black Belt." Johnathan threw a towel at me.

"He gave my grills away," I continued to mope.

"And when I walked in, you had a colander on his head.

I think you scared the poor guy to death."

I got tickled at the thought of that. I couldn't hold a grudge with Johnathan around.

"I'm going to take a bath. Promise not to leave me alone with him tomorrow."

"I'll wear some armor and I'll come running when I hear the dishes flying."

"Will you look in on Jason and Kevin for me?" I asked.

"Done. Go take a bath. I'll try to get the ribs away from Barney. I'm sure he won't let Tommy back in the kitchen with all that food in there."

He got up to leave.

"I'll pay you if you leave Barney in there for another hour," I offered hopefully. He chuckled and left.

When I woke up, I felt panicked. I tried to remember what it was I had to do. Oh God, the party. Why in the hell did I want a barbecue? My grills and meat. I jumped out of the bed and fell over Barney. I looked at the clock. Shit, I had overslept. Why hadn't Johnathan gotten me up?

I had fifty things to do at once. I brushed my teeth, swiped at my hair, and threw on my old jogging pants and ever-present T-shirt. This one threatened "Screw With Me and Die!" One of my favorites.

I flew down the stairs, Barney took this as a cue to play and attacked me as I bounced down each step. He had part of my shirt in his mouth as I marched into the kitchen—his little bit of a tail wagging happily. The kitchen was quiet and Tommy wasn't there. I looked on the table. I was shocked. The frozen waffles were made. Orange juice. Real orange juice, not papaya or guava. There was real syrup. Oh joy of joys. Johnathan must have made breakfast. Now I know why I love him.

Jason and Kevin came in and looked around. Jason was suspicious. He sniffed at the juice, "What is this?"

"Breakfast."

"What did you do with Tommy?" He looked at me accusingly.

"Buried him with the grills," I gleefully quipped.

Kevin's eyes widened "Neat. Can I stay for the party, Mrs. Jesse?"

I liked this kid. "Sure, just call your mom to see if it's okay with her. Jason, I need you to cut some flowers for me out of the garden and don't butcher them. Just cut them."

"Do I get to use a knife?" Jason asked his eyes lighting up.

"No, I want you to chew them off." I smiled at him, reaching over to tussle his hair. He ducked out of my reach and slammed out the back door.

I carried my coffee to the den. I needed to dust, then vacuum, and clean the bathrooms. Great. Barney was slurping water out of the toilet. When he finished, he looked at me for approval.

Three hours later the house was shining. Having company was hell. No sign of Tommy anywhere. I was winning the war.

I opened the cabinet to get the serving dishes out. Nothing there. Odd. I opened the other cabinets in a frenzy. No dishes. I tore open the silverware drawer. No forks and no spoons.

Nothing. I ran to the refrigerator. My meat was gone. I would kill him.

I ran to the door and started bellowing, "Tommy, you little son of a bitch. Bring me my meat."

When Johnathan got to me, I was foaming at the mouth.

"What is the matter with you, Jesse?"

"My meat. He stole my meat and the dishes."

"Who?"

"TOMMY!" I screamed.

"Honey, calm down. I'll find him and your meat. If I don't, I'll call a caterer."

"The damn dishes too! Johnathan, everyone will be here in two hours and I'm not dressed. What am I going to do?"

"We will handle it. Where's Jason?"

"Oh God, I sent him to cut flowers hours ago."

I ran back to the kitchen. Jason had flowers everywhere, only they were still attached to the roots. He had dirt in every vase.

"What did you do?" I gasped in disbelief.

"You said not to use the knife, so I pulled them up."

"Oh God, look at all the dirt. Johnathan do something!"

What was that humming noise I was hearing? Maybe my brain was burning out from all the stress. I went to the back door; it was Vernon in his helicopter. What was he doing? He made a low swing at the house, circled, and zoomed off towards his house.

Back to pressing matters. Jonathan had taken Jason and Kevin in search of Tommy. I looked around at the dirt on the counters and floor and thought of my ruined cook out. Sweat was pouring off me now. I had to go take another shower.

As I stood under the shower with the hot water going full blast, I was hoping to find more information about the murder at the party. Maybe find out if Dirth had died of natural causes. Hmm and I had to take that stupid anger class that J.P. had thought up. A few minutes later I slipped into new jeans and ironed a T-shirt for the special occasion. This one declares, "Jesse is a Goddess." I heard the doorbell ringing. Must be the caterers. I pulled on the knob of the bedroom door. It didn't open.

What in the hell was wrong with the door now? I got a better grip on it and pulled harder. This is ridiculous, I thought.

I went to the intercom and pushed on it. "Jason, Jonathan, somebody, answer me now! The door won't open, I need to get out."

This was getting too weird. I knew Tommy could get vengeful, but this was way out of line. I looked at my door and kicked viciously close to the handle. The wood around the handle splintered and the doorknob fell on the floor. I think I broke my foot with that kick. I pulled the door open.

As I limped to the rear of the house, I heard music coming from the speakers at the pool. What was going on? There were candles lit. Bright white linen cloth covered the tables. There were yellow roses in silver vases on each table. There was a wicker shack in the corner that would serve as the bar. The party had started. Jane, Sasha, and Al Smith had gathered in a group and were talking—God only knew about what. I heard Mac's voice booming over the music. He was slapping Ken on the back. Barney had Crystal cornered by the bar. Tommy, wearing a starched white uniform, came out with a tray loaded with wonderful looking food.

"Tommy, what's all this?" I asked quietly.

"Chinese Spareribs." He looked at me defiantly. "My specialty."

Jane picked that moment to swoop down on me. She had on navy walking shorts, with a nautical striped blouse—her hair perfect as usual.

"Jesse, my dear, I never knew you had such fabulous live-in help. Thomas has been keeping us quite amused while you were being tardy."

"Yes well, Thomas as you put it, has a way about him that is quite unique. He is a real prize. Aren't you, Thomas?" I cooed.

"I bring more food." Tommy made a small bow at Sasha and left. I was speechless. I walked with Jane and Sasha over to the bar and asked the bartender, also an Oriental, whom I had never seen before, for a very large glass of wine. Yes, I had definitely lost control somewhere, I thought.

"Get this damn dog away from me, " Crystal hissed. I called Barney. He reluctantly came over to my side.

"Having a good time, Crystal? I assume you have met everyone, while I was being tardy."

"Yes, I know everyone here. What's wrong with you?" Crystal asked.

"I don't know. I feel as if I have been in the twilight zone. Have you seen Johnathan around?"

"Do I look like a tour guide to you? She had her ever present coffee cup in her hand. Sometimes I think she had it surgically implanted there. In fact, we may all be better off if she just walked around with an I. V. in her arm dripping just the right amount of caffeine into her veins. I turned back to Ben Glasglow.

"Hi, I'm Jesse Statham. I took your class in college, but I'm sure you had so many students you couldn't possibly remember me."

Mr. Glasglow was as round as he was tall. He did not look like I had remembered. He had on a baby blue pair of linen pants and matching western shirt. What hair he did have left was almost white. The only strange things on him were a giant diamond ring and a gleaming gold Rolex.

"My, of course, I remember you and your wit which you were well known for around the campus."

So he remembered. I was impressed. "I am flattered that you still know who I am. Would you care for something to drink?"

"Yes, I'll have bourbon and bourbon. No water, it takes away from the taste. I like my drinks strong and true, as God intended them to be."

Okay, I thought, would you like a funnel with that? "No problem, just help yourself."

Ken swaggered past Mac and made a beeline for me. He was dressed in his day-on-the-ranch gear, aviator sunglasses, tight jeans, fitted denim shirt, and brand new lizard cowboy boots, his long blonde hair pulled back into the usual ponytail.

"Jesse!" he screamed.

"Ken!" I echoed.

"When do we ride?"

I looked at him closer. Damn, if he didn't have a new pair of riding gloves in his hand, and the ever-present cellular phone.

"We eat first, swim, then ride if everyone would like to."

Sasha had been quiet long enough. Jane was talking about her horse.

"I wish he was here today so I could ride him," Sasha announced.

Everyone turned and stared at her, including Jane.

Sasha was decked out in her usual solid black, only today it was shorts and a matching top. She had to be wearing a wonder bra, nobody's breasts could stand up that straight.

"Sasha," I pointed out, "Classy isn't a horse that you ride on a trail. He is a harness racer, a champion one at that."

"I know that, silly. I was just thinking that it would be fun for him," she snickered.

Crystal and Ken rolled their eyes at the same time.

"Anybody ready for Tommy's wonderful food?" Jonathan questioned from behind the bar.

Everyone wandered back to the beautiful tables surrounding the pool.

"What happened to you?" I asked without moving my lips.

"Tommy and I came to an agreement. Don't worry about a thing."

I continued to smile. "Were you aware that I was locked in the damn bedroom and had to kick the door down to get to my own party?"

"My oak door?" Johnathan moaned.

"My right foot, but I'm fine. Thanks for asking."

"You smashed another door down. Jesse, those doors are hard to come by, and they don't make them like that anymore."

"Again, thank you for your concern."

Tommy came walking out followed by Asian people I had never seen before. Each person held a giant Pu Pu platter with a small inferno burning in the middle.

I turned to Anna. She was looking in the direction of Jane Glasglow with a strange look on her face.

"Anna?" I gently whispered.

She slowly turned to me and I caught just a hint of total hatred in her eyes.

"Yes?"

"Are you all right?"

"I'm as all right as I can be under the circumstances. If you will excuse me, I need to go to the powder room." She pushed her chair back and stomped off.

"What do you make of that look?" Crystal asked. She was still munching on the shrimp.

"I don't know. Damn, don't you ever get full?"

"Well, excuse the hell out of me. I thought this was a barbecue."

"It is but have you considered going to the front pasture and just grazing?"

Crystal didn't look up. "Did you take your hormone pill?"

"Yes, damn it, and I am getting tired of hearing that same question all over town."

"Well, get a clue," she griped. I hate her.

"May I get in on this charming conversation?" Mac sat down.

"She is in a mood, Mac." Crystal warned him.

"She always gets this way under stress. Remember the time at Christmas when she decided to entertain formally and had to wear high heels? Before the night was over she had fallen of them three different times. Boy, was she miffed," he jabbed grinning.

I was becoming tired of this. I just smiled at them and pretended they didn't exist. I still couldn't figure out what to do about Jane and Smith. I had to get them separated for a while.

I leaned over to Mac and whispered, "How about going over to Jane and sucking up to her so I can talk to Smith alone for a few minutes?" He raised his eyebrows but nodded at me.

Before he could get up, Tommy appeared with his grand finale. Again it was on fire, sort of a Chinese version of a baked Alaska. It was huge and sat on a silver platter with fortune cookies sticking out everywhere. The crust was down right sinful. Tommy escorted the dessert to a side bar and with a flourish bowed to me.

Everyone gathered around to get a plateful of the gooey treat when I heard it. A helicopter. Vernon. He wouldn't dare. He put the helicopter down almost on top of the pool. Tables started flying; I could hear people yelling. The water from the pool was coming up at everyone like a tidal wave. I could see Vernon through the windshield. He held the chopper over the pool for a few minutes and took off. I would kill him and soon.

I looked around. Sasha's hair was standing straight up and she was sobbing. Jane Glasglow had taken the most direct hit from Tommy's dessert. It was all over her. Her face was covered in white. Jason and the other kid were in shock. Barney was busy licking the food off the cement and barking. Tommy was furious. One of the umbrellas had landed on him and he was stuck under it. I don't know what he was saying but he was cussing a blue streak. Mac had gone over to help Crystal. She was clutching a rib in her hand. Everyone was either wet or sticky or both. My neighborhood had become deranged. How was I ever going to explain all of this? Where in the hell was Jonathan?

"Jason, go find Jonathan, now; tell him to call the police out here right now." I reached over and snatched up a table its umbrella hanging limply to the side.

I walked over to Jane. She was wiping sauce off her face. "Jane, I am so sorry about all this."

She was having none of it. "What in the hell is wrong with you people? I came here for a cookout and wind up with Sushi and an Air Show attack." She was wiping furiously at her now messed up clothes.

"Jane, as I was saying, I don't know what could have possibly caused my neighbor to behave like this, but be assured I am calling the police."

Tommy was standing next to me now. He whispered, "He air raids because you shoot him in butt, what do you mean about Sushi? That Japanese not Chinese."

"Whatever, Asian dish it was, it was horrible. I have had enough. Come on Al, Ben; we are leaving."

I was ready to scream, you can hate my meat and me, but damned if you are going to insult Tommy, even if I do hate him at this minute. Instead, I reached out to Jane and pushed her in the pool. Then Tommy shoved Ben in and Mac grabbed Smith by the collar and tossed him in. Sasha looked around and grabbed Crystal. Crystal didn't let go so they both landed in the pool with a splash. Jane surfaced spewing water. Miraculously, she started laughing; then everyone started laughing and choking on water.

Jane squinted up at me. "Well at least you're loyal even if you do throw a strange party."

I reached my hand out to her to help her. Big mistake. Miss athlete pulled and I went in headfirst. Damn, this was fun. Jason came running out followed by Johnathan who looked at me questioningly.

"Since when do we go swimming in our clothes?"

"Just today, honey, why don't you help me out?" Before he could, Jason shoved him in and followed suit.

We were all splashing around in the pool by now. Johnathan had saved the day by making strong drinks for everyone.

After about an hour of fun, I announced it was time for the trail ride. Everyone took a different room to dry off. I was having a hard time getting my wet jeans off. They were on like glue, the more I tugged, the more determined they were to stay on. Just when I was thinking of getting Johnathan's blowtorch out to burn the damn things off, Crystal strode in and grinned an eat shit grin. "Are we gaining weight again?"

"Crystal, shut up and help me."

"Why should I? I enjoy seeing you suffer." She grabbed the bottom of my soggy jeans and almost threw me on the floor. I screamed and struggled like a snake shedding skin.

"For God's sake, Jesse, you act like you just gave birth to something," she exploded.

"What part of shut up didn't you get the first time?" I retorted.

Crystal continued, "I really don't want to go on a trail ride, you know."

I reached into my drawer to pull out yet another pair of jeans.

"So? Your point is?"

"I don't like horses like you do; they scare me."

"Crystal, all you have to do is learn to bond with them."

"I don't want to bond with them. I like my animals tall, dark, and handsome." She was serious.

"Well, Flazon should be perfect for you, he meets all of your requirements," I smiled at her.

She stuck her tongue out as we strode out to join the others.

Barney loves a trail ride. He decides at the beginning that running ahead of the horses and flushing out birds is a good thing for my heart condition. Prince, as usual, was determined to be first and Flazon stuck his nose up Prince's butt. That is a no, no on a trail ride. I also don't like people riding next to me, since on a trail ride it is common for unfamiliar horses to try and cow kick one another. Sometimes the aim is off, and I have had an ankle broken with my foot in the stirrup.

I turned back to Crystal who had a death grip on the horn of her saddle and suggested, "Pull him back a little, he's too close to Prince."

"No," she whispered.

"Why not?"

"Not my problem." She continued to hang on to the horn.

"Okay." I pressed my legs lightly into Prince. He took off trotting. Flazon has a very rough trot. Unless you know how to post to the trot, you are going to have one hell of a bumpy ride.

Crystal screamed, "Jesse, stop! You're killing me. I'll get out of your horse's butt if you will just make him walk."

I slowed Prince. By then everyone was on a horse and looking pretty good except for Sasha and Smith. Sasha was on Mac's horse Baby, a gentle soul. Mac had put Smith on Shadow, a mean black Morgan mare. Under saddle she was perfect, but on the ground she would try to kill you. Another one of my abused animal finds. I couldn't have picked out a better ride for him myself.

Jane was on a huge gray thoroughbred that looked like a tank cutting a path through the trees. She seemed to know what she was doing. She sat in the seat well—toes up, heels down, back straight. She also had a light hand. Someone had paid for a lot of lessons.

Prince decided to take me between two pine trees before I knew what was happening. He almost managed to knock my kneecaps off again. Naturally, Flazon had to do what Prince had done. I could hear Crystal screaming as she left part of her skin on the trees. I stopped and motioned for everyone to go around me while I tightened my cinch.

I really wanted to ride next to Smith, and since he was lagging in the back, I decided to join him. He was looking green around the gills by then. His horse Shadow had her ears laid flat back. Not a good sign. I rode up beside him.

"You doing all right?" I inquired. Like I cared.

"What is wrong with this horse, is she mean?" he asked shakily.

"Nah. She's a real sweetheart under saddle." I drawled. Well I wasn't lying; she is good under a saddle.

I decided to take the bull by the horns. "Are you planning to reopen your practice any time soon?"

"No." he bluntly responded. "I decided I have had enough of the small animal routine; from now on I intend to do race track visits. More money."

"You remember F.I.?" I inquired. "Well, he said the damnedest thing to me the other day. About Classy."

He looked at me. "Oh and what interesting thing did my esteemed colleague have to say?"

We were at the end of the pack and they were heading for Jason's clearing, his place when he needs solitude.

"Well, he was just talking about the insides of a horse not exactly matching the outside. What do you make of that? I asked eyebrows raised.

"I don't know. He could just be getting a little senile. I have an appointment with your boss Monday morning to look into becoming your insurance company's veterinarian."

I almost fell out of my saddle. Over my dead body would that happen. Or his.

"Smith, I met your son the other day at the super market. Nice kid. He also had a lot to say."

He stiffened in the saddle making Shadow crow hop to the left. "Why did you bother my son? You really should watch where you snoop, Mrs. Statham."

I opened my mouth to give a reply when I swallowed a gnat. I swear Georgia gnats have to be on steroids. When you swallow one, all of a sudden you are full. Then they were everywhere. The yellow flies joined them. I had had enough.

I clucked to Prince and we took off at a canter. I knew Shadow would follow. She did. Jason took this as a sign to take off like a bat out of hell across the power line. The Power Company keeps the line open for miles. It is great for riding.

The only ones not faring well were Sasha and Smith. Mac and Johnathan had taken off after Jason and Kevin. After running for a few minutes to get the kinks out, I remembered Ken. Where was he? This whole thing had started because of him. I knew he had ridden off with us, but I hadn't seen him since.

I turned Prince around and decided to backtrack and see if I could spot Ken. It didn't take long. He had stopped his horse; he was still on it—on his cellular phone. That has to be a first for me. I mean how can you bond with nature and be on a phone at the same time? I eased Prince closer to him.

I heard, "Look, I'm doing all I can at this point. I thought I was supposed to have a little help on this end. Yeah, right. How am I supposed to learn what they're up to by following them around?" He looked up and caught a glance at Prince and me.

He stiffened. "I have to go, bye." He stuck the thing back into his pocket. "Jesse, how long have you been there?"

"Long enough, Ken. Come on it's time to go back. By the way who was so important that you had to make a call from horse back?"

"Oh, just my Dad. He is having trouble, you know."

"No, Ken, I don't know. Why don't you tell me something I'll believe?"

He looked stricken. Of course, he always looks stricken. "I can't believe you are talking to me like that, Jess."

"Believe it. Ken. I threw this shindig for you, and you aren't even courteous enough to act halfway interested."

"I am interested. What can I do to make it up to you? I also noticed the way you keep quizzing Jane Glasglow. What is going on there?"

"You notice too much, Ken. Let's put the horses up." Everyone was at the barn by then. Smith was retching next to the barn.

"What is wrong with him?" I asked Johnathan.

"Shadow."

"What did she do?"

"Seems that when you disappeared, she decided she had had enough and brought Smith back to the barn in under two minutes. She clamped that hard mouth of hers down over that mild snaffle you insist everyone use, and he couldn't control her."

"So?"

"So, then she ran straight into the barn with him on back of her, and when she got to her stall, she locked it down and Smith was eyeball to eyeball with her. Then he kind of fell off."

"Damn, he gets upset easy, doesn't he?" I smiled and pulled the saddle off Prince.

Back at the house everyone was saying good-bye. I didn't think they would ever leave. I love company, but about an hour is all I can take.

I found Johnathan in the den. He was reading the paper. "You learn anything today, Dolls?"

"Not much. I think Ken's up to something though. Oh yeah, Doctor shit wad thinks he is going to work for my insurance company."

He chuckled, "This should be good."

"I'm going to kill Vernon." I announced.

"Seems to me that if you would leave him alone, maybe he would leave you alone."

"Your logic sucks as usual," I retaliated.

"No it doesn't," he said softly.

"You don't understand. No one has ever taken up for me. I have always had to do it. Therefore, it just makes sense that I need to kill Vernon."

Johnathan put the paper down. "I take up for you."

"If it's a matter of life and damn death, you do, but not for the Vernons of the world, you don't. Your whole family is dysfunctional as hell."

He looked at me as though I had gone crazy. "Mine? Just because we don't think you should go around and shoot people because they fly down our driveway, that makes my family weird?"

"Yes, I'm glad to see you finally understand."

He kissed me on the forehead and muttered something about giving up.

I went to the kitchen where Tommy had straightened everything up. He is a very tidy person. I found what I was looking for. I yelled to Johnathan that I would be back later and marched to the van with Barney in hot pursuit.

I drove to the back of the barn and parked the van where it couldn't be seen. Then Barney and I snuck into the woods. In the clearing stood Vernon's pride and joy. His penis extender. The helicopter. I finally found the gas tank and proceeded to pour a five-pound bag of sugar in, and for good measure, I kicked the side panel. Maybe it's Freudian, as if I was really kicking him in the balls since his helicopter is part of his anatomy. Happily, Barney and I slipped back through the woods to the van and on to the house.

Chapter Ten

I slept like a baby that night. Who says revenge can't be good for one's soul. As the sun rose, I pried one eye open and realized that there was a wet tongue on my neck. It wasn't Jonathan's. Barney had put his gorgeous head on Johnathan's pillow and was slurping wet kisses all over my face; I love wake up kisses. He was in a good mood, too because as I slung my feet to the floor, he signaled that he wanted to wrestle. We lunged at each other and I was on my knees growling at him. I am Alpha; he is Beta, whatever that means. After twenty minutes of much needed bonding, I gave him one final hug and inched my way into the shower.

I was standing under the hard spray of water when I remembered what Smith had said about working for Equine Casualty. Well, there went my day, and I scrubbed harder with my loofa. I have to be the cleanest detective I have ever met.

The shirt of the day was a mild one. It read simply, "If you want to live, then don't speak to me."

Barney and I trotted to the kitchen. It was deserted. I opened a can of Supreme dog food for Barney and wondered if Tommy had made coffee, and grabbed the paper off the table. On page three was an announcement about Smith starting a large animal practice. This was not good. The house was quiet so Johnathan had gotten Jason off to school. I checked my blood sugar level imaging that the finger I had to stick with a needle was Al Smith's face. I adjusted the insulin level on my pump, pulled out the bottle of regular insulin I take when my blood sugar is up and then loaded the syringe and popped the shot in to my arm. I whistled to Barney and we hustled to the office.

Sasha was waiting on us not looking happy at all. She had on her power red Nancy Reagan suit. She held a pencil in her hand like a weapon.

"Morning, Sasha, " I managed to edge past her desk. Even Barney held his little nubby tail a bit lower.

"Some morning, Jesse. That bitch Rhonda is back."

My blood froze. Maybe I had misunderstood her. "Did you say Rhonda?"

"Yes, the one and only." As she finished the sentence, I heard the pencil snap in half. Sasha reached down and picked up another one.

"Where is Rhonda?" I asked.

"Oh she is unpacking in HER new office next to Ronald Live's. You know the one that is someday to be mine. If you hadn't beat him up and your dog hadn't bitten him, I would have had that job. Not her." Another snap rang out.

Rhonda was a sore spot with Sasha and me. She had been let go and fired for lack of a better term two years ago for under the table dealings. Never proven, of course. She is much too slick for that.

Was I ever going to get through this karma thing? Ever since Rhonda had left, Sasha had tried everything known to mankind and insurance kind to land her job. This would not be pretty. She reached for another pencil.

"Okay, Sasha, back away from the desk slowly. We will handle this together. Now put the pencils down," I urged.

She looked at me as if I had lost my mind. "I will not back away from my damn desk and I will handle this myself." With that she snapped the last pencil, turned, and slammed the desk drawer shut.

Barney and I shuffled into my office; he lay down in his spot. I turned Rod Stewart on medium since I had to think. I lit a red candle and a white one. It couldn't hurt. Okay, what was happening to my insurance company? My life? First, I get a new boss, and then Smith decides to work here, then Rhonda? No way in hell all that is a coincidence.

Besides I don't believe in them. Then I had to take into consideration Jane, her husband, Smith, Dirth. Oh God! Anna! I forgot Dirt's memorial service.

I blew out the candles, snapped the leash on Barney, and smiled lovingly to Sasha as we hurried to the van.

The power queen stopped our departure with a look from hell. J.P. was standing just outside the door arms crossed, dressed in a brilliant hot pink tailored suit. I felt the need to put my sunglasses on the color was so bright. Her mixture of diamonds and jeweled clanging bracelets would never make it undercover. J.P glanced down at Barney, then back to me.

"Jesse, I have some wonderful news for you. I managed to move your anger management class to today, and they have a new art therapy that I believe would benefit you."

"J.P., today is out. I have to go to Dirt's, um Dirth's memorial service. Sorry." Ha. I had her there. Let her beat that excuse.

She reached to stroke Barney, blinding me as the bracelet clashed down her arm. "Sure you can, Jesse. I have great faith in your ability to do several things at one time. Don't forget I allow you to bring Barney to work in spite of the state law that prohibits him from being here." She smiled at me.

"But Georgia," you bitch, I thought, "That means I'll have to dress three damn times today. I don't know if I'm stable enough to handle that."

Turning from me she called over her shoulder. "Do it. Starts at six p.m. sharp. Same place as last time."

Damn, damn, damn. Fine, I would do the damn therapy. I was probably angry from putting up with the boss from hell. However, I make good money and I can dress like I want, but changing clothes three friggin' times in one day. Ugh. "Maybe a bus will hit me," I said to Barney.

I high tailed it back to the house, found my black funeral pantsuit, and slapped it on. Couldn't find any lipstick so I went into Jason's room, found finger paint, and smeared it on. Then I remembered food. I had to take something, so I flew into the kitchen and looked in the refrigerator. Nothing, just cabinets and boxes. I looked into the wooden container on the countertop. It was full of fortune cookies. Shit! They would have to do. I grabbed a big bread basket, rammed a napkin into the bottom, dumped the cookies in, and told God I was sorry I was such an awful person. I was at Anna's twenty minutes later.

I had on my black pumps; you know the ones that are supposed to allow you to play basketball in them. Shoe ads lie. I slipped on gravel the whole way up to Anna's porch, my toes jammed into the bottom of them like sausages. Yeah, rush me to the basketball court. People swathed in black swarmed around the porch. God, this was sad. Not that Dirth was dead, but knowing people only put nice clothes on at funerals was a sad thought. Maybe Sasha was right and I needed to dress up more. Nah. I must be losing my sanity. There were small kids playing tag quietly next to a big oak tree. Why do people drag their kids out to this kind of crap? Can't they just let them be young? There is plenty of time for this later. I mumbled my way through the door to find Anna.

The gathering looked like a trainer convention. Every trainer I had ever heard of was there. Most were older, sun-baked, their skin proving that they didn't believe in sun block. Several had their stable caps on with their colors proudly displayed. They may be from all over the world, but they were still a family. Most of them owned the horses they trained, slept with them, and traveled with them. Some own two, others forty, but they all had one thing in common, their love of horses. They get up at three in the morning, feed, brush, pick hooves out, examine the horse, and start training at five. At nine in the morning training is finished, stalls already mucked out. At that time they break for a snack. Then all the horses get a bath, brushed again, and finally a blanket. While the horses rest, these wizened old timers break down all the equipment they used that morning and piece by piece wash and clean it. Every day. When they finish and everything is in tiptop shape, they feed at least two more times that day and take temperatures. Then these horse lovers stand around and shoot the shit. I know several mothers of children who couldn't take that routine for long.

Anna appeared, wearing a long flowing black gauzy thing. She was pale, probably from all the people running around her house. I'm also certain she was tired of people asking, "How are you?" I didn't know what to say. Glad your abuser is dead didn't seem appropriate. She took my hand in hers. She was ice cold. I wondered if she had low blood pressure.

"Jesse, thanks for coming. There is plenty of food in the dining room." I shoved the cookies at her giving her a long, sympathetic look.

"Anna, if you need anything, please call me." I moved into the dining room and ran smack into F.I. He had a chicken leg in his hand and deviled eggs in a little plate he was holding.

"Well, F.I., I can see you are overcome with grief," I pointed to his plate.

"Yea, sure am, seems a shame that Dirth had to go that way."

"What way?" I asked.

He popped a deviled egg in. "Poison."

"Poison, nobody said anything about poison to me. When did this come up?"

"Jess, you're not supposed to scream at people at funerals, keep your voice down to a holler." He grinned at me.

"You have been snooping haven't you, F.I.?"

He responded, "Heard all about your fancy shin ding too. You really know how to throw a party."

I got closer to him and lowered my voice." Okay, little man, unless you want that chicken leg rammed all the way down your throat, you had better start talking, and I don't mean maybe."

"Now, now Jess, I'm getting around to it. Still on that hormone blocker? Anyway, as you know my brother-in-law is the coroner after all. He may have mentioned something to me about his autopsy coming back with a strange drug in the tox screen."

"What kind of drug?"

"Paronyl."

"What in the hell is Paronyl? Was it for his heart?" I sputtered.

"Nope." God, trying to get him to talk today was like having a root canal, so I stomped on his foot.

"What in the hell did you do that for, Jesse?"

"I just wanted to see if you could actually say a whole sentence without taking another bite of food."

"Well," he glared, "just for that I'm not telling you the rest." He took another egg off his plate.

I hissed, "Are you addicted to cholesterol? Now what's the rest of it?"

F.I. averted his eyes toward the front hall. "Look who just walked in, Jessica."

I turned toward the front. It was none other than Vernon. What in the hell was Vietnam's answer to *Silence of the Lamb* doing here? I had to know. I stood next to F. I. and watched as Vernon slithered his six-foot-four wiry frame across to Anna.

How did he know her? Vernon greeted Anna with a cool nod of the head. She took his hand in hers and intimately embraced him. Even F.I. stopped chewing for a few seconds. He had a piece of Swiss cheese in his hand. Why do people pay money for cheese with holes in it? Vernon was still holding Anna's hand when he looked straight at me. He dropped her hand. I smiled at him, my I bet your Mother wished she had aborted you smile. Vernon worked his way around the room.

He eventually made it to me. "Jesse," Vernon stated.

"What?" I looked up at him.

"Just making conversation," he replied without a smile on his face.

"Why?"

"Thought I would be social."

"Again, I vex the question, why?" I was now eye to eye with him.

"Dirth and I were friends. Not that it's any of your business." He sneered reaching for the coffeepot. He poured himself a cup and stared at me.

I couldn't help myself. I picked up the silver dish. "Sugar?" I asked innocently.

Vernon almost spit his coffee out. "I know that was you, Jesse."

"What?" I asked pretending shock.

"You put sugar in my helicopter." He was sneering again.

"Someone put sugar in your helicopter, Vernon?" F.I. asked.

Vernon's face contorted, "You know damn well she did it, Doc."

"Can you prove it, Vernon, or did you just dream it?" I asked.

"You better keep a close eye on that mangy dog of yours before something happens to him," he threatened.

I blew. "Anything happens to Barney and I will fucking kill your family and burn your damn helicopter to the ground, you piece of crap. By the way, how is your butt?"

He slammed his coffee cup down splashing coffee everywhere and gave me his meanest glare. I glared back.

F. I. stepped in "Remember, son, she's just crazy enough to carry out that threat, so if I were you, I would take it seriously." Vernon stomped off.

F.I. gave a sad shake of his head. "Jesse, you are never going to learn anything if you don't quit threatening people. You should know that by now."

"F.I., I can't help it. He should fall off the face of the earth he's such a shit. Plus he threatened Barney. You heard that part I know."

"I didn't say I don't blame you. Just try to keep from telling people exactly how you feel is all," he picked up another chicken leg.

Anna began making her way over to us. Her hair looked like Loretta Lynn's. That country look certain women like. They can't bear to cut their hair even though they desperately need to. Anna really couldn't make up her mind about having bangs or not, so she wore a half bang heavily moussed. She waltzed up with black fabric flowing behind her. I noticed F.I. had quit sucking on his chicken leg.

She spoke in her quiet voice, "Thank you so much for coming." She looked at us as if expecting clever words from the Muses.

"Wouldn't have missed it for anything in the world." I gushed. That didn't come out right.

"Your secretary didn't come with you, I see. Sorry I couldn't stay long at your party Jesse but, other things had to be attended to." Anna replied, smoothing over my screw up. God, she was gracious.

"No problem, someone had to stay at the office."

"Sasha was so fond of Dirth," Anna announced.

I jerked my head up. "She was?"

"They were together all the time. On the phone, of course."

"Of course." What in the hell was she talking about? Sasha barely knew the man.

"We sure are sorry about your loss, Anna." F.I. inserted.

"When was the last time you saw Dirth?" I questioned.

"It was the morning he died, at breakfast." Anna's bottom lip trembled.

"Did he mention anything out of the way to you?"

She paused a minute. "As a matter of fact, he mentioned that Jane Glasglow had sent him a copy of the papers on Classy. Of course, all that is void because of his death."

"Not necessarily, Anna."

Anna's eyes narrowed, "What do you mean, Jesse."

"Just that in Georgia the law is a little vague on ownership if a party dies within forty-eight hours."

"Can't you look into it? I mean there has to be something you can do to help me."

"I take it that you don't want Jane Glasglow to get her hands on Classy."

She looked determined. "I will do whatever it takes to see that that doesn't happen."

Conveniently Pastor Walker walked up. He is the headmaster of Jason's school. He was a horse person also and wore a cross of two spurs soldered together around his neck. Anna abruptly excused herself and walked off with him.

I needed to look into little Anna's past. I had a feeling everything you saw wasn't what you thought it was. I felt someone pulling on my sleeve. Crystal and Ken had arrived. I wondered if they were together.

Crystal couldn't contain herself any longer, "Jesse, you're not going to believe what I just overheard. Jane was standing over in the corner with Smith talking about my newspaper."

"Well, what did she say about it?"

"That she wants to buy it." Crystal disclosed leaning toward me, raising a heavily penciled eyebrow.

"She doesn't have that kind of money," F.I. interjected.

"I didn't know the paper was for sale," I admitted.

"I didn't either, and I am very pissed off about this so called funeral. I mean, my God, why is everyone so sad? It isn't like anyone actually liked the son of a bitch," Crystal emphasized.

"Crystal, try to get back to what you heard, "I coaxed.

"That's it. You know, Jesse, when I die I want everyone to do an apathy on me." All three heads turned to look at her.

"You mean a eulogy. All right, I'll do it. What do you want me to say? That at funerals you went around bitching about how you hated other people's funerals. I know, I'll get Barney to be a pall bearer."

She spat out, "You had better not let that damn dog near my body when I die."

Out of the corner of my eye I noticed that Ken had left us to go over to the huge mahogany dining table to consume food and mingle near the other mourners. He had spotted Tommy's fortune cookie mound in the middle of the table. Oh God, I hope Tommy hadn't put weird sayings in them.

"Jesse, are you paying attention to me?" Crystal nudged me with her hand.

"Yes, Crystal, I am. I think I pretty much have your death covered. You want lots of animals and speakers at your funeral."

"Can we please change the subject now?" F. I. had quit gnawing on his chicken leg.

"F. I., I want you to please tell me more about the autopsy," I begged.

"What autopsy?" Crystal practically screamed.

Everyone had gotten quiet by now. Jane was looking over at us a broken cookie in her hand. She marched up to us.

"Is this some kind of sick joke?" Jane hissed.

"What?" I asked.

"This. This damn message in the cookie." She thrust the paper toward me. I felt apprehensive. I didn't want to take the piece of paper. Crystal beat me to it, snatching it out of Jane's hand. I could see her face contorting as she read it.

Crystal looked her straight in the eye." So, how does this concern us?"

I was dying to know what it said, but I just stood there. Jane glared back at Crystal a full five seconds before she turned on her six-inch high heels and walked off.

"Okay, Crystal, what did it say?" I asked pensively.

"Oh just something about a guilty consciousness needs no accuser."

"Great, Tommy probably sits up nights composing these sayings. I didn't have anything else to bring." I was looking for a little sympathy. None was forthcoming.

"It wouldn't kill you to have a casserole in the freezer for these kinds of things. I know even at my busiest I always manage to get a few extras frozen, for you know, tragic events," Crystal snipped.

I hate her. She is so damn organized. Christ, even her clothes are ironed a week in advance. I do not believe that this is the sign of a normal person.

As usual, I couldn't find Ken and wondered what he was up to.

"Are we supposed to go to the church now?" I asked Crystal.

"No, Jess, Anna is having a memorial at the house, the burial or whatever she chooses to do with him is family only."

"How do you know so much about what she's going to do with Dirt?"

"Because I work at the newspaper, fool. I think I'm going to get a bite to eat if there is anything left."

"Jesse, quit biting your lip." F.I. warned.

"I am in deep thought, Doc. I have never been in a room with so many people with ulterior motives before. It seems like a vulture convention. Damn, I don't even have a clue who I should be watching."

"Don't cuss," he warned.

"Sorry. Are you ever going to finish telling me about the poison?"

"What part of it do you want me to repeat?"

"You were telling me that Dirt was murdered?"

"That's right."

"Well, out of all these wonderful people here, who do you think would want that to happen? I mean besides me?"

"You need to look into Hartman's finances, Jess."

"What is that supposed to mean? Have you heard something? What do you make out of Jane's attempt to purchase both a horse and a newspaper in the same week? Plus the fact that you had to charcoal tube Classy right before Jane bought him?"

"Exactly."

"Exactly what, F.I.?"

"You are too suspicious, Jess. Just try to quit suspecting everyone in the room for a minute."

"If I do that, what am I supposed to do?" I protested.

"Go get a chicken leg. Mingle. Quit growling at people," F.I. suggested.

"All right I can do that, but I can't help it if all these people act like they have something to hide. Look who just walked in." It was Ben Glasgow.

F.I. groaned, "I give up."

I stuck my tongue out at him and walked over to Crystal who was in deep conversation with a woman I had seen before but didn't know. She was definitely Crystal's type— solid black dress, huge matching hat. I wondered if someone was cloning Sasha.

I cleared my throat. "Hi, I'm Jesse Statham."

Crystal introduced, "Jesse, this is Star."

"Star of what?" I asked.

"No, that's my name,"

"Must be hell to live up to." I smiled at her.

"Not at all, I'm quite good at it," her voice tinkled. I had never heard anyone's voice tinkle before. I was impressed.

"Did you know Dirth well?"

"Yes, we were well aquatinted. I'm Anna's sister. Younger."

"Of course, you live around here?"

"Not far from here, I'm staying with Anna to help her through this."

"I don't remember seeing you before, but you look familiar…"

She interrupted, "Oh, but I have watched your career unfold for awhile. I have either read or heard of your-shall we say adventures. You have gotten mixed up in some pretty serious stuff, haven't you? I mean a couple of months ago it was all over the news about how you found out some people had electrocuted a horse, and when the police got there, you had given the two people shock treatments with the cord of a lamp."

"Oh that, well, stuff happens," I said, trying not to smile.

"I heard it took the swat team to finally convince you to untie them. Have they sued you yet?"

"Matter of fact, yes, they have."

"Did they win?"

"No," Crystal put in. "Jesse has a guardian angel looking after her wherever she goes."

"Right. How long will you to be in town, Star?" I inquired still thinking the name was strange.

Her slender wrist waved the air as she said, "I haven't decided yet, but let's be sure to get together before I go back."

"That would be great, maybe we could have lunch?" I offered.

"Not without me, you don't," Crystal put in.

"Crystal, how long is this thing supposed to last?" I whispered after Star had turned to talk to the pastor.

"Don't go to many memorials do we, Jesse?"

I hate her. "No, we don't. There are some things I'm dying to get home and look up."

"On that strange computer of yours, no doubt."

"You are just jealous that my modem is faster than yours."

"At least, I can type with all my fingers, unlike you," Crystal responded.

"I can't help it if I got thrown out of typing class in school."

"If I remember right, you hit a boy in class up side the head with your type writer for pulling on your hair," she smirked.

"I have worn it short ever since and you have modem envy," I pointed out.

"Look who just walked in." I looked. Sasha and Jason entered with Barney on a leash, which was a sight I didn't see often. What were they doing here? Something had to be wrong. I waved at Sasha. Jason had started talking to the trainers. I didn't need this. Barney was dragging Sasha toward the food. All those months of dog obedience out the window.

Barney sniffed me out of the crowd wagging his nubby tail a hundred miles an hour. God, I love him. He is so regal. Sasha and Jason cut through my worship of Barney.

"What is it?" I hissed at Jason.

"Hey, Jess, Sasha made us come here. I was in school and she pulled me out of class for a funeral. Oh yeah, you need to sign a pass for me. I know you're tired, don't bother to read it first. I know how your eyes hurt when you get older."

Ignoring him for the time being, I looked at Sasha. She was dressed to the hilt only I didn't know whose black hat was larger, hers or Star's.

Sasha started, "My therapist said I should do more things like this and quit hiding from them. Jason called from school, so I went down and picked him up. But before I could leave the office, Tommy came trotting in with Barney. He said you were expecting him. Did I do all right? Plus, that bitch Rhonda is coming, so naturally I had to get here before she did."

"Hello, Jane." Sasha cooed tossing me Barney's leash before she took off toward the Glasglows,

I looked at Crystal. "I just want to know when she had time to go change clothes and grab the hat."

Jason was over at the buffet table passing Tommy's cookies around. Barney started growling softly. This was not a good sign.

I looked in the direction Barney was looking. Ronald Live. What in the hell was he doing here? Mr. Evil himself. Was anybody left at the office? Behind him stood Rhonda.

I reached down and patted Barney's head to quiet him. I watched Rhonda and Live walk through the room together. Sasha would have a stroke. Boy, this was a happening funeral or wake or memorial, whatever Crystal chooses to call it. Everyone I could think of was here including Barney. Personally I was getting tired of seeing these people, I mean first at work, then socially, then at my party. The only person missing was Mac. I figured he would be here in a few minutes. Thank God, Johnathan was working.

All of a sudden there was music blasting through the house. "Cool, Hootie and the Blowfish." Jason exclaimed. I looked at him closely. He hated Rod Stewart but loved Hootie. Go Figure. The song was "Running from the Devil." How appropriate.

Barney was pulling on the leash to go toward the table. I stood my ground and told him, " No." He looked suicidal again. I guess I need to put him back on Prozac. Ronald Live finally made his way over to us with Rhonda in tow. Rhonda is an anorexic looking, willowy Clairol number 76 from Eckerd's redhead, who wears a "I ate the last piece of cheesecake then puked it up" look on her face.

"Mr. Live, what brings you here?"

"I didn't know I needed to clear my schedule with you, Ms. Statham."

"Well, you do."

"What?" He was shocked.

"I said you do. Did you know the deceased personally?" Sasha had maneuvered over to my right side. Barney was between us growling.

I continued. "Why is Rhonda here and did you know Dirth Hartman personally or not? I want to know now." I thought, you slimy little person.

"You can't talk to me like that."

"Yes, I can. I inherited and have made a lot of money, so I really don't have to work. I choose to; therefore, I can do whatever I want."

He glared up at me because I am at least a foot taller than he is.

"I will have your job for this outburst, Ms. Statham." Barney continued to growl.

I quietly said. "Promises, promises, I want to know how you knew the victim? Also explain to me why Rhonda is working in my building. She must really be working hard for you." Just then Hootie started singing a song about time.

"I don't have to explain a damn thing to you. Come on, Rhonda; we will go somewhere less crowded."

"Damn, Jesse, what got into you?" Sasha's jaw had dropped to the floor.

"Sasha, I have just about reached the end of my rope with that man. For some reason he really pisses me off. Besides, Barney doesn't like him."

"Good enough reason." Crystal put in. "Also a good way to lose your job, Jesse. What's the matter with you?"

"I don't know. I think I'm very premenstrual. Oh hell, Cooper is here."

I grabbed Crystal by the arm, grabbed Barney's leash, and sprinted toward the back of the house.

Star and Sasha tackled Cooper at the same time. I don't see how the two hats didn't collide. It got very dark in that corner of the house, sort of like a locust invasion. It had to be the hats. He hadn't stood a chance.

I darted into the kitchen where Crystal stood with an open bottle of wine.

"Here, drink this." She said.

"No glass?"

"Drink, damn it. Why is it I can't even go to a funeral without you turning it into a free for all?" She leaned against the counter while I passed the bottle back to her. She took a slug. "God, Jesse, my marriage is in trouble."

I looked at her. Not again. "Are you serious?"

"Yes, we never do anything together anymore. All he wants to do is sleep on the couch. He doesn't like anything I do. You know I joined that archaeological society."

"The Indian thing."

"Yes. He won't even take me to look for rocks."

"Do you think he's having an affair?"

"Hell no. I give him sex whenever he wants it." She said as if that solved everything.

"What has that got to do with an affair, Crystal?" I mean I did try to hide the fact that Frank was a jerk who had crawled out from under a rock. But if that made her happy, I could live with it.

"I am just not happy with him anymore. He is either hateful or gone."

I took the bottle back. God, this was going to be a long day.

"Have you thought about counseling?"

"He won't go." How surprising. Him being such a jewel and all.

"What are you going to do, Crystal?" I asked knowing the answer was nothing.

"Don't worry about it, Jesse. I'll handle it." Barney had put his head in Crystal's hand and she was stroking him. I knew she had lost it.

I heard Anna's voice announcing in the living room. There was no more piercing Hootie. Ken was standing next to Cooper smiling. What was he up to? Anna was saying something about how nice it was that we came and basically now to get out so she could go cremate Dirth. Damn, that's the one part I would have enjoyed—burning Dirt.

Everyone stood in line to say goodbye, asking if Anna needed anything and telling her how sad that she had lost her husband. I just looked at her. She seemed calm to me, almost serene.

I loaded Jason and Barney into the van and headed home. I felt sad. How unlike me.

Chapter Eleven

When I got home, Barney jumped out to mark at least fifteen trees with his scent. I don't know why he doesn't dehydrate from all the peeing. I half expected Jason to follow suit. Instead, he put a piece of paper in front of me before I could unbuckle my seat belt.

"Here, sign here." He had also managed to produce an ink pen.

"Jason, I would appreciate it if this could wait until I have at least had a chance to get in the house."

"You don't need to worry about all that, just sign."

"Can't."

"Why not?"

"Seems that when old age took my eye sight, it also gave me arthritis so my hand won't work.

"Well, sign with your left." He was sharp.

"Can't."

"Why?"

"Same problem." I deadpanned.

"Damn. Both hands?"

"Yeah, don't cuss."

"Sorry, well make an X. Can you do that?"

"With what? My teeth?"

"That'll work, yeah."

"No it won't." I reached out and snatched the paper out of his hand. He started screaming, "Give it back." I glared at him and he quit.

The situation was not good. Seems like Jason had decided to turn into an arsonist at school. I was shocked at this. I kind of thought in all the time he had lived with me that we had gone though most of the adolescent crap. I was wrong. Jason, according to the paper, had tried to burn down the bathroom at school. I looked at his black hair and beautiful innocent brown eyes. He is so cute.

"We will discuss this after dinner." I promised searching his eyes.

"Am I in trouble?" he asked.

"Big time would be more appropriate. Maybe we need to take a look at the military school."

"I am innocent, see you at dinner." He quickly hopped out of the van.

I drug myself into the den. I needed a drink, so I made a martini on the rocks—very little vermouth. As I was savoring the four olives I had slipped in, Tommy came into the room.

"What?" I snapped.

"I just want to see how your day is." He leaned against the door arms folded in front of him.

"No, you don't, now what in the hell do you want from me? And thanks a lot for taking Barney to Sasha and if I get a nasty fortune cookie tonight, I may turn your ass over to that Chinese gang that is looking for you."

"How you know about that?" He was very still.

"I have my ways, so don't start something or I'll throw your skinny Asian butt all over the house."

"Tommy is insulted." He announced.

I doubted that. "Good. What do you want?"

"It can wait," he mumbled.

"What can wait, and why are you drinking martinis before dinner?" Johnathan was home. Thank God.

"Went to memorial service. Crystal's talking divorce and Jason's an arsonist, and I have to change clothes AGAIN for another anger class," I said chewing on an olive.

"That all?" Johnathan answered. "Well Barney chewed another rope off of my pile of new post again. What is with him and his need to own all the rope he comes across."

"He loves his rope is that a crime? Besides, I think he is very talented. Could somebody please give me a little sympathy or I swear I will shoot someone," I threatened.

"Honey, I'll give you sympathy. How about a hug instead of alcohol?"

"Are you crazy? Nowhere near the same. I need this to calm me." And God help anyone stupid enough to try and take it away from me. I continued to suck at the olives. Tommy had sat down on the end of the couch and folded his hands in his lap as he closely studied me.

"You wind up at Betty Ford."

I gave him my most withering look and asked, "Tommy, why do you always think I need detox?"

"If it not cough syrup, it's wine, not wine, gin. Put together," Tommy reasoned.

"Bite me."

"Tommy need to talk to you about problem." He was looking toward Johnathan.

"Okay," I said getting off the sofa. "You have my full attention. What is it?"

"I need couple days off."

"Why?" I asked.

"I not question you when you have to do things, this very personal. Okay?" I continued to look at him.

He stared straight back at me.

"All right, if you need to take time off, go ahead. When will you be back?"

"Be back Friday." As far as he was concerned that was that. Jonathan had gotten up and was pulling money from his wallet.

"Here, Tommy, take a few hundred with you in case you need it. Take a credit card too." He handed both to Tommy.

Tommy had stood up rigid as a board. "Can't take your money, Mr. Johnathan."

"Yes you can, Tommy, you work hard around here; think of it as a bonus." Tommy looked at me. I was flabbergasted. Johnathan had never been one to hand over money, especially a credit card without laying down the rules first. All I could do was nod yes.

"I leave tonight. That okay?"

Not with me. "Where are you going? At least tell me what state."

"I call you." Tommy left the room, his head held up proudly. That was that.

"Johnathan, what was that all about?"

"I think it was something that meant a lot to him and that we should respect his privacy. Lord knows he doesn't get any around here."

"What in the hell is that supposed to mean? I give him privacy," I yelled.

"Jesse, you are on call twenty-four hours seven days a week. That means this house is on call too. Whenever you decide to go chase someone, or research stuff night and day, you are always yelling around here at the top of your lungs, flying through the house. Then there is Jason. You try to replace his mother, Then there's Barney, the horses, your friends and their problems." He paused.

"And your point would be what?" I fired back.

"Honey, you know I don't care what you do as long as you are happy and safe. But to Tommy and the rest of the world, you are like a tornado. If something's broke, come hell or high water, you are determined to fix it."

"That so bad?"

"There's no bad to it. That's just the way you are. Plus your hormones. The doctor said for you to slow down a little."

That pissed me off. "Don't you dare bring my hormones into this. God, a woman can't have one little hot flash without everyone going nuts. God, Johnathan, you really are a dysfunctional person. I'm so sorry I am not as damn calm and brain dead as you are. I'm going to get ready for class now so don't hold dinner."

Barney was in the bathroom with me as I was running the water into the tub. All of a sudden I started crying. I couldn't stop. What was wrong with me? Okay, maybe Johnathan was right and I needed to be easier with people. No. That was not possible; he was never right. Shit. Life could be hard. What was I going to do about Jason? Dirth? I have a new boss I had pissed off too. Maybe I did need to call my doctor about adjusting my dosage. I sat in the floor clinging to Barney and bawled like a baby. He started howling. Johnathan ran in and looked at us.

"Dolls. What can I do to help?"

"Shoot me."

"Anything less permanent than that?"

"No, I ask one small favor and you won't do it," I blubbered.

"22 or 32?" Johnathan asked, that mischievous gleam in his eyes.

I hated him. I bit my lip and clenched my jaw to keep my face straight. I hate it when I'm upset and he makes me laugh. Barney was waiting for a sign to continue to howl, bite the hell out of Johnathan, or pretend he was joyous to see him after five minutes. Finally, I cracked up laughing. I changed into a T-shirt plain white no saying on it and left.

The class was held in the bottom of the hospital basement next to the Alcoholics Anonymous group. Next door as I made my way through the haze of smoke massive silver coffee urn and paper coffee cups that the AA's were gathered around, I went past another door with people screaming their hearts out. I instinctively drew my gun out and held it in against my chest as I cautiously looked in the window in the door. At least twenty people were armed with foam bats beating the hell out of each other. Primal scream therapy, I thought, putting my forty-five into in my bag.

I found the door I was looking for and slowly walked in making myself breathe slowly. There were several large tables with steel chairs around them. Nine people were spread out sitting in small groups at the tables. On the tables lay huge pads of white paper and containers of crayons. Oh God, I thought, what were we supposed to do? Stick the crayons up our nose? Or I could probably ram one into someone's ear.

A beautiful ebony skinned woman dressed in a white linen dress approached me and welcomed, "You must be Jesse. I am Amy. Please have a seat wherever you want."

I scanned the room seeing mostly blonde women and one brunette mixed with three men. I chose the brunette. She had a short shagged haircut, and was dressed in a two piece canary pant suit with rhinestones all over the front of the shirt that did a pretty good job of hiding her two hundred pounds.

The three men wore an assortment of plaid shirts and lime green or baby blue pants. They must have just walked off a golf course. Golf rage? I wondered if all of the bright clothing everyone but I had on possibly explained the anger thing, I know if I had to look at them very long, I would become violent or ill, or both. It was like being at a parrot convention. The brunette looked me up and down smacking gum with enthusiasm. "I'm Chartreuse."

"Jesus," I moaned shoving a hand through my hair.

Amy interrupted us, "Okay class, I would like you to draw your favorite things on the art pads and use any colors of crayon you want. You have ten minutes; then I will talk to you about your work."

I looked around. Most of the class was working like beavers.

I picked up a black crayon frowned at it and pensively started to outline my favorite things. Barney, Johnathan, Jason, guns and knives and tennis balls. After ten minutes of nonstop drawing, we were instructed by Amy to stop.

"Now class, I will look at your drawings." She moved to the blonde glee club trio table. Amy reached down and held up a drawing with a house, car, and two kids playing in the yard and a small woman gazing down from an upstairs window.

"Okay class, here we see a single parent with low self esteem depressed over the fact she can't pay for her car and wishes she had had two abortions."

"Jesus, how in the hell did you come up with this one." I wondered out loud.

Chartreuse whispered. "That must be one angry bitch, huh, Jesus, she didn't draw no flowers or nothin."

Amy moved to the next picture, this one of a house full of people and one small woman outside the house peering from behind a tree.

"Here we have someone who is full of rage. Notice how she has removed herself from the family in the house and the person is hiding behind a tree which means she is hiding her hatred of her family. A ticking time bomb."

I squirmed in my hard chair as Amy made her way to our table. I leaned down, crossed my arms, and tried to hide the drawing from her. Didn't work. Amy snatched it up and frowned, "Jesse, this is very different." She held the drawing toward the class. "Jesse has no people in this picture, so she does not admit she exists. Only her weapons are there for her. You are a lonely person and you have built several walls that you refuse to let anyone in, and, for some strange reason, you enjoy tennis." She kept tapping the picture of the tennis ball with her tapered nail and chewed her bottom lip as the therapist in her studied me.

Chartreuse chimed in. "I think Jesus is in denial. And she does like sports."

I was ready to blow but tried to appear calm as I slowly stood up and towered over the teacher. "Fine I have walls and, yes, I enjoy weapons because they do serve a purpose in my line of work. For example, a plumber has wrenches and a painter has brushes and a ladder, so I have weapons. However, the tennis ball is for filling with gasoline and rolling under a running car at a red light. When the ball ignites, it causes a small blast." I turned to the open-mouthed Chartreuse, her hundred pound eyes wide, "The name is JESSE, not Jesus, but I can see how you would confuse the two. I will see you kind people next week as I have thoroughly enjoyed this class." I grabbed the duffel bag, flipped them the bird, and walked out.

I passed back through the screaming class into the haze of smoke when I heard someone say, "Jesse, I knew you would be the first one out." It was J.P. Double shit.

Chapter Twelve

"J.P., did you just finish your AA meeting?" I smiled sweetly.

"Very funny, Jesse." She fell into step with me going into the parking lot. "Where are you going now?"

"Why, you wanna date?" I was still pissed off at the stupid class.

J.P. straightened her mandarin orange blazer and glared at me.

"This is important, Jesse, I heard through the grapevine that Al Smith is involved in an Alabama horse farm. What do you make of that?"

I looked at my black leather strapped Timex watch, "I think I shall go and visit the jerk."

I was opening the van when J.P. walked to the other side.

"I think I should go with you," she announced slamming the door and sliding into Barney's seat. Damn, okay if she wanted to go fine but I was not going to be nice about it.

Traffic was heavy as I drove, J.P. directing me to where Smith lived. I grinned as I made my way to the swanky apartment Smith rented. Sasha lived in the same complex.

J.P. reached over to turn down my Tina Turner music.

I barely moved my mouth as I snarled, "Touch it and I will break your damn skinny arm."

J.P. settled back putting her fingers in her ears as I swerved into the parking lot on two wheels.

"Love your driving, Jesse. Didn't you once crew for Richard Petty?"

The woman would not shut up as we walked into the glitzy lobby. "I am so glad you attended all of those anger management classes. I can tell all of the money I have put into you is working. You are not nearly as abusive as you were last year. Remember when I had to call in a favor from Judge Kelly because you pistol whipped the man who suffocated his horse by holding a plastic bag over his head. Yep, you are one cool cookie now."

We had arrived at Smith's apartment door. I put my ear to the door holding up a hand to stop J.P. from coming closer.

"Jesse, what in the hell are you doing? Ring the bell."

"Shut up, J.P. Damn, I can't hear anything with you talking as though you have overdosed on cocaine. I don't think he's here."

"When did you become a damn Indian tracker?" She pushed the doorbell. Nothing happened.

"I told you he wasn't here," I gloated, taking my case of lock picks from my duffel bag.

J.P. groaned as she eyed me taking a pick out and working on the lock. "We can not break into his house, Jesse."

I continued to work the pick. Damn, I wish she would settle down. She's like a hummingbird tonight. No wonder I have anger.

"I am not breaking into anything, J.P. I am being a good citizen because I could have sworn I heard him calling for help. Here we are," I announced as I opened the door.

I peered around the corner of the door scanning the barely furnished open living room and kitchen combo. What I saw was all white: the walls, sofa, wing chair, and carpet. Lots of tacky glass and gold tables around. Mr. Personality's domain. I took a step in and J.P. rammed into me. I jumped.

"Damn, J.P. could you make a little more noise?" I whispered.

She narrowed her eyes and said. "Jesse there is no one here and now we have broken God knows how many laws, and you want ME to be quiet?"

I didn't answer as I quickly searched the hall closet.

"You think he is hiding from us?" Damn, she could be a pain.

I rolled my eyes at her and made my way down the hall into a master bedroom, which contained a circular bed with mirrors overhead.

Caroline, F.I.'s new assistant at the animal clinic, was lying on the bed with a trickle of blood coming from the small hole in the center of her forehead.

"Holy shit, Jesse, she's dead."

God, she is such a genius. I walked over to the young woman and put my finger on her neck. I swept my eyes over the small figure of about twenty and her white uniform twisted around her waist, with her long black hair laid out on a pillow her eyes staring at us.

J.P. brushed me out of the way, "My God, Jess, her pulse is not where a horse's would be."

"Fine, I don't think she's dead, but I wonder what Caroline was doing here?"

"She can't be alive, Jesse; she has a bullet hole in her head."

"It's a small caliber hole J.P., maybe a twenty two, not exactly a gun to kill yourself with."

She looked at me strangely. "Might I ask why not? A damn bullet is a bullet."

I started rummaging through Al Smith's desk. "Not necessarily, I know of several people who have attempted suicide with a twenty-two and didn't die. On the other hand, it is a caliber an assassin would use. You know the old saying about twenty twos. They are like roaches; they go into roach motels and don't come out." I pulled out another pick to pry open the locked drawer. Meanwhile J.P. had taken her compact out of her purse and stuck the mirror under Caroline's nose.

"J.P., are you checking to see if she's a vampire?" I smirked.

"Hmm nothing, are you finished with your ammunition lecture, Jesse?" She snapped the compact shut. "What are you doing to that desk? Your concern for the poor girl is overwhelming, I think we should call the police."

I smacked the damn drawer harder and it gave. "Just give me a few minutes more."

J.P. started to sit on the corner of the bed.

"Don't contaminate the crime scene," I yelled at her.

"So it's fine if you rip the door off, fling open the closet, and rip the desk open but I can't sit down?"

"Well, no you can't. Besides all I did was touch her neck when I checked for a pulse."

"You never cease to astound me, Jesse. Just because the poor woman does not have hooves, she is inconsequential to you? You know her?"

I was leafing through papers and nodded at her. J.P. had gotten up and tucked the phone under her jaw calling 911, I assumed.

I continued to snoop and turned up a paper with Ben Glasglow's signature on it and was trying to read it when I heard the front door open. I knew I had shut it after we had entered. I jumped up, stuffed the papers into my pants, and shoved an open mouthed J.P. into the closet with me. I pushed her into the corner of the massive closet where she landed on top of a pile of clothes and linens. That was the last glimpse I got of her as I shut the door and the darkness hit us.

I held my breath as I heard someone approach the bedroom. Then screaming started. I recognized the scream, Sasha!

I swung the closet door open and drug Sasha into the closet and ordered, "Sasha, shit be quiet, I hear someone else coming in." Sasha whimpered, but I couldn't make out her words

I pulled the switchblade out of the pocket of my jeans and hit the lock to open it, the sound it made was as loud as a clap of thunder. I craned my neck to see out of the small slit in the closet door. All I could see was tanned flesh. As Al Smith yanked the door open, I spilled out onto the floor. I am so graceful at times.

"Ms. Statham, you killed Caroline Hensonblan." He was red in the face, I hoped he would have a stroke. As I tried to get up, he kicked me in the chest sending me reeling against the desk. I dropped the switchblade and he quickly grabbed it.

I lay against the desk waiting to see what kind of fighter he was. If he moved fast, he was not that good. On the other hand, if he moved slowly, which he was, that meant he was pretty damn decisive about which move he would make. He approached slowly twirling the knife, a hateful gleam in his eyes and smiled down at me.

I pretended I was hurt badly still clutching my chest where the asshole had planted his foot. "Smith, you killed her."

"Can you prove it? This is my apartment and I definitely do not remember inviting you in. So if I kill you, hypothetically, it would be self-defense."

He had his back to the closet. I smiled up at him while watching J.P. sneak out of the closet holding her two-shot stainless-steel derringer tightly.

"You would know how to carve me up wouldn't you, Smith? You being a veterinarian and all or did you get your degree through a correspondence course?"

Just as he started to lunge, J.P. barked, "Move away from her, Smith, or I will blow two holes in you."

Smith whirled toward J.P. as I jumped up and side kicked the knife out of his hand. Sasha came out screaming like a banshee wielding a golf club she must have found in the closet and smashed him in the leg. I heard an explosion. J.P. shot him in the foot. I whirled and gave him my best roundhouse kick to his face. Damn, we are good.

Cooper and his men in blue rushed us and we all fell on the corpse in a tangle with Cooper on top of me. I couldn't help it. I said, "I knew you wanted me all this time."

We were handcuffed, thrown into a paddy wagon, and hauled down to the police station. No one was very happy as we sat in Cooper's office in a semi circle around his desk while he tapped his ink pen against his head. Maybe he will knock himself out, I thought.

J.P. spoke, "Lt. Cooper I think you have misunderstood our position at Dr. Smith's apartment." She was rubbing her wrists where the cuffs had been. Mine were still on. This ought to be good. I sincerely hoped she would point the crone's finger at him because she swears that it is capable of withering genitals and rendering them totally useless from then on. Luckily for him, she didn't as he continued to beat his brains out as he answered her.

"As I see your position, Ms. Lee, you are suspected of murder, firing an unregistered gun, and assault on Dr. Smith, not to mention breaking and entering. Did I leave out anything?" He looked straight at me.

I shrugged my shoulders. "Hey, all I did was go to art class. I am a perfectly innocent bystander who you tried to mate with on the bed on top of a dead person. You really are sick, Cooper."

He stopped pounding his head.

"I did not, Statham!"

"Did too. In fact, I saw you light a cigarette afterwards. You know, when we were thrown into the wagon like convicts."

Sasha sat in the only decent chair in the room pouting prettily at Cooper.

"Jesse is just kidding, Mike. I know it was me you were after." She looked down at her black silk housecoat with matching fuzzy sandals and back to my shirt and jeans. Oh brother, I thought, she's serious.

J.P. cleared her throat. "Lt. Cooper surely we can come to some sort of agreement to keep this incident out of the papers."

I interrupted her, "Look charge us or release us. I want a lawyer now and take these damn cuffs off of me." I glared in Smith's direction. The real murderer has HIS off."

Smith's head was bandaged and the tip of one of his loafers was gone where J.P. had shot his shoe off. He had a little blood on his preppy tan alligator shirt. His nose had tape on it where I had landed a kick. What a wuss! I supposed he needed Tylenol.

"I am the injured party here, I demand that that woman be locked away," Smith spoke trying to look superior in his chair.

"You talkin' to me?" I asked in my best Robert DeNiro imitation.

Smith tried to come at me, but Cooper blocked him.

I jumped up in my Tae Kwon Do stance. "Bring it on, little man."

Cooper shoved me back into my chair. "STOP IT!"

Everyone grew quiet as he called in four more policemen to watch over us.

There was a knock at the door. Three men and two women entered, the legal eagles from Equine Fidelity. I looked at J.P. in amazement; how in the hell had she gotten the lawyers here so fast. The room was now filled to capacity with people.

Everyone was talking at once. Smith was screaming, "Lawsuit."

I screamed, "Police abuse" just for the hell of it and J.P. screamed at the lawyers who were very calm. Guess they were just happy to have something to do until Ben and Jane Glasglow arrived. When they finally did, Jane in an expensive silver running suit informed us that her husband was Dr. Dick head's lawyer.

I pointed out, "If that is the case, get Barney down here this minute to represent me." I also demanded to see my one true love and friend in the department, Captain Lonnie. That made everyone shut up. By now Cooper was beating his head with his hand as though trying to clear his ears of fluid. At the rate he was doing this, I calculated he'd knock himself out in an hour. Or at least give himself one hell of a concussion.

Suddenly, Cooper screamed, "I give the fuck up."

Sasha had found chips and a coke somewhere. Pig.

I suspected that my blood sugar had bottomed out and frantically called out, "Someone, find juice or sugar before I go into a coma." I continued, "Or we can sit here all night and I can sue everyone in here for malpractice and inhumane treatment of a prisoner."

Chocolate bars were pelted at me along with sugar packets, one ding-dong, and a Diet Coke. That last one had to be a smart-ass since there isn't any sugar in Diet Cokes.

The door opened again and Captain Lonnie appeared all six-six feet of mean dark muscle, a stern expression on his handsome face.

He scanned the room not speaking. His eyes found me as I, still handcuffed, shoved a ding-dong down my throat. I smiled at him. He winked at me, then quietly instructed the lawyers to go to another room. Next, he adamantly advised Cooper to uncuff me.

I snarled at Cooper as he attempted the command, "Do not fuck with me until I finish the damn ding-dong." I kept the cuffs on. Captain Lonnie looked at me seriously, "Jesse, are you all right?"

I nodded, yes, still chewing.

"Your blood sugar drop?"

The sweat had started to stop, turning me cold, another wonderful thing diabetics get to enjoy. Now if you want the ultimate reaction stopper actually worth taking extra insulin for, just ask for Baklava. "Yes, Lonnie, I'm fine, but I would feel better if you put the cuffs back on Dr. Dickhead; he scares me."

Lonnie grinned and patted my shoulder as I rose from the floor. He walked over to Smith and slapped on the cuffs before the idiot could take a breath. Smith glanced down as if hallucinating and began sputtering. Lonnie raised a hand and Smith quieted.

Captain Lonnie Blesser had loved me ever since I had saved his wife. Three jerks had attacked her at one of the stables where I had been and between him and me, we had kicked some redneck ass. That is another story, but it was nice to have one policeman here who cut me a little slack.

Cooper glared at me. "You are not leaving until I get answers."

"Ask away." I swallowed the rest of the Diet Coke. "Lt. Cooper, you know I always try to be helpful to you," I lied.

Cooper's face was red as he smacked the beloved pen on the desk like he was a drummer.

"Statham, what were you doing at Dr. Smith's apartment? A little b and e perhaps?" He whirled the pen in the air catching it behind his back. He was demonic or maybe he was practicing for a circus.

I leaned forward in my chair, my cuffed hands pointing to J.P. and Sasha.

"We were invited."

One Hell of a Mystery

Cooper dropped his pen in mid air. "What?" I don't believe that, Statham."

I held eye contact. "We were invited by Sasha. We do all work together, you remember?"

J.P. jumped in. "That's right, lieutenant." Cooper looked incredulously at J.P. and me.

I inserted, "We were at Sasha's going over paperwork when we heard a scream."

Smith cut in. "Bullshit."

I stared him down. "Let me finish, Dr. Quack."

"Make her stop insulting my integrity," he sniffed.

I deadpanned, "What integrity? Anyway, we heard a scream and Sasha, J.P., and I went to check it out. It came from apartment 411. We did not realize that it was leased to Dr. Death.

Lonnie was leaning against the door smiling and asked, "Jesse, how did Dr. Death, uh, the doctor, here find you?"

I shifted in the hard ass chair. "Well, after we went into the unknown apartment, J.P. called 911 and we heard a noise, so naturally, we hid being women with a dead woman, we, uh, we were afraid." I bit down hard on my bottom lip and tasted blood. God, I couldn't start laughing now.

"How did you get in the door, Statham?" Cooper was back to the pen Olympics.

"It opened when I turned the knob," Sasha said.

"Yeah," J.P. agreed.

"Then when we hid in the closet from the killer Dr. Deranged, who started beating the hell out of me," I embellished.

"He did. He hit Jesse and I hit him with a golf club. Ms. Lee pulled out her pretty little gun to try and make him stop."

"An antique," J.P. offered.

I finished, "Then Cooper came in and threw us on top of the victim and made us ride in a paddy wagon while he drove Dr. Dud in his comfortable car.

Lonnie looked at Cooper, who reluctantly allowed us to go home.

Chapter Thirteen

When I woke up at seven, I didn't want to get out of bed. There was this real feeling of dread in the pit of my stomach. I'm never like this. What was wrong with me? Then I remembered, Tommy was gone and the police station last night. Guess I needed to go make breakfast, not the most challenging thing in the world to do.

I was in the kitchen wrestling open a can of frozen orange stuff after having put the frozen waffles in the toaster. This isn't so bad, I thought until the white plastic decided to give only a micro inch at a time. Finally all my efforts paid off. I had the plastic ripped off. Then the container fell out of my hand onto the floor, a frozen orange popsicle in a wreck. About that time both fire alarms went off as I turned to see the waffles incinerate like a flash fire. Jason and Jonathan ran into the room.

"God, she's cooking again," Jason announced, sarcasm dripping.

"Honey, we can just eat cereal."

I glared at Johnathan and bent down to scoop up the frozen Tang from hell.

"We will be like *Leave It to Beaver* if it kills us," I retorted.

"Leave it to who? I have a feeling it will kill us," Jason said.

I reached into the fridge and pulled out cheese and crackers. I stomped to the microwave and nuked the plate of food. Then I sliced some bananas, stuck a toothpick through them, and shoved the plate on the table and announced, " Breakfast is served."

"You mean we have to eat hors d'oeuvres, Jesse?" Jason asked in awe.

"Yes, it's a wonderful way to start your day. Enjoy. I'm going take a shower. By the way I'm taking you to school, so be ready when I come back. Johnathan I need to see you for a minute."

In addition, I needed to check on Anna and Jane's backgrounds today. I figured I might get lucky and run into Star, too.

Johnathan followed me into the den his large forty-ounce glass of ice tea with him. I told him about Caroline's body and the police station incident.

He listened as he sipped his tea and replied, "mmmm." Which in Johnathan language means, "you poor thing I hope you will be fine is there anything I can do? Please take care of yourself, I love you. Now I am off to work, I hope you have a great day you sexy woman."

After I dropped Jason off at school, I headed for the securities building. I finally found a parking space after using my middle finger until it cramped flipping people off.

The government building was huge with marble stairs and floor. The temperature was ten degrees colder inside. So many people with their business suits on going briskly through the halls. You would have thought by their mannerisms that they were in some secret society that didn't allow them to speak, much less look anyone in the eye. Anne Klein would have been proud.

I turned the corner following some of the suit herd and ran into an old friend of mine. Carter is six five and 180 pounds of rock hard steel. If you have heard of AB's of steel, this guy has balls of iron. I hadn't seen him in awhile. He is a little on the paranoid side, was once a Navy Seal, and is into marshal arts. However, he isn't as good as I am. His hair was shorter than usual and he had a serious look on his face. Carter used to do work for me at the insurance company when I needed muscle. Now he is, of all things, a personal security tactical expert, which is nothing more than a bodyguard for the rich. He reached out, grabbed me, and lifted me in the air.

"Jess, it's been too long."

"Put me down, fool." I screeched, struggling to get out of his arms. "What are you doing here? One of the rich and famous get into trouble?"

He grinned at me but for only a second. He doesn't like for anyone to see him smile. I think that he thinks that smiling makes him look younger.

"Just between you and me, Jess, I'm here for damage control of sorts."

"Who and what kind of trouble?"

"Can't give names just a hint. From what I hear through the grapevine, she is not one of your admirers," he smirked.

"Imagine that. Someone doesn't like me. I am devastated."

"Yeah, right. Let's get together for coffee after I am finished here and we can catch up on old times."

"Like the time you were on surveillance and the kid threw a smurf football at your undercover van and you tried to shoot him. Okay, I'm game. Meet me at the front at five," I grinned.

I had news for Rambo. I intended to follow his ass all over the building until I found out, not only who he was working for, but what kind of damage control he had to repair.

Carter started in the records department. I went into the adjoining glassed in office and started my search on Anna. I looked at files on insurance mortgages and school loans until my eyeballs were about ready to burst.

Finally Carter moved to the tax office. What was he up to? I followed. He went directly to the computer in the back of the office. There was a very perky blonde about two feet tall who looked at me over her desk and asked, "Can I help you, ma'am?"

I didn't want to be noticed that soon, but since she was so short, I hadn't seen her.

"No, thank you. I was just going to make sure I had paid my taxes for the year."

"Which ones?"

"Oh, uh, county," I stammered.

"I'll check for you, won't take a minute. Name?"

"Hartman, Anna." What had made me say that?

"Just a sec." She trotted to the desk where she whipped into action by slam dunking her monitor around to face her. Reminded me of that girl's head in the *Exorcist*.

In five seconds as promised, she exclaimed, "Aha."

"Aha what?" I asked.

"Looks like you missed the trash dump tax and naturally there is a penalty for that."

"What trash tax are you referring to? The one at the ranch?"

"No ma'am, the one out at the place you own near the river."

"I forgot. My husband just passed away and he always handled this type of thing. In fact, I'm so scattered brain right now I can't seem to remember the address. Dumb me." I tapped my head with my index finger.

"No problem. That would be 525 North Side Circle, Sentinel Farms. From the size of the bill, you must use the refuse container a lot."

"I'll be right back. I need to go get my checkbook. I am so absent minded today." I backed out slowly toward the glass door.

I backed right into Smith, Dr. Prick. His head was still bandaged, his lip swollen from my roundhouse kick. Life can be so great some days. I wondered if his foot hurt, gee I hope so.

"Jesse Statham, what are you doing here?"

"Just checking on a few public records. You?" You satanist, I thought.

"Came down to make sure that my license was still valid."

"Is it?"

"Of course. Why wouldn't it be?" He looked at me through narrowed hateful eyes.

"Well, I do know several people who would argue that point with you. Starting with me." I was watching his body language. He had taken a step back and had folded his arms together. I continued to stare him down.

"I really would watch my back if I were you bitch." he said coldly.

"Oh please I am so terrified of you, please don't hurt me I beg of you. Oh, by the way, you man me woman, have you been out to the place on the West Side lately, somewhere near Northside Circle?" A blank expression came across his face. Then he messed up. I saw the corner of his mouth twitch.

"I don't know what you are talking about." He pushed past me in the direction of records limping I noticed with pleasure.

Why had I blurted that out to him? I am totally losing it. I felt something grab my arm. I turned and hit the person in the throat with my elbow. There is one advantage to being tall. You have long arms. I looked up at Carter standing there holding his throat and coughing. I do enjoy torturing him.

"Sorry, I thought you were Al Smith. Are you all right?"

"You knew damn well it was me, Jesse." He was glaring now still holding his throat.

"You know better than to sneak up on me like that."

"Guess you haven't taken the hormone blocker today."

"Cute, real cute. What did you find in records?"

"I would share with you if you hadn't hit me in the throat."

"All right I will buy your damn lunch to get you over it and for that I expect some kind of sharing of the souls."

He followed me in his armored van, in case there was a shoot out in the traffic he would survive and make it to a free lunch.

We went to the same Italian restaurant that Ken and I frequent. For one so gung-ho about the simple life, Carter sure has expensive tastes. Mr. Personality, the maitre d' met us.

"Madam, I see you have regained your eyesight," he said sarcastically.

"It is a miracle. My sight has been pretty good the last couple of days. Now we need a table," I smiled at him.

"Do you have a reservation?"

"Of course." I lied "Would I be here if I didn't?" All but three tables were empty. This man hated women. He obviously was not breast-fed at birth.

Finally, after eyeballing us for at least thirty-seconds, Maurice, the waiter of the year, pointed to a table next to the kitchen door. I ignored him turned to the left and sat down at a table for eight.

I watched as Carter consumed every dry bread stick in the place I watched; he crunched. I also noticed he had a weird way of holding his napkin. First, he picked it up; then he folded it over twice and wiped the corners of his mouth. I had never seen anyone so neatly handle linen.

Maurice strolled over to take our order. Carter decided what we needed was a steak and lobster. I didn't care what he got as long as I could get him to talk. Naturally, he had to have iced tea and water and coffee and cappuccino. He had to have a bladder the size of Montana.

"Okay, Jesse, what was with you finding Dirth Hartman's body?" He continued to munch.

"Jealous?" I inquired.

"God, you're not going to do the penis envy thing again, are you?"

"As long as you don't do the uterus thing, I'll try to restrain myself."

He leaned back in his chair and looked around the room casually. I know that look. It is called Hi Low. He could surveillance a room full of people and every damn corner where a bomb or camera might be before the salad arrived. He was always tense. He could look casual, but his eyes were always very intense. I knew that if anything looked out of place or moved wrong, he would be on it in a New York minute.

"So, Jesse, what was with the two red necks you beat the hell out of the other day? Were they connected to Hartman's death?"

I slammed my water glass down and looked at him. "Nosy, aren't we? I just want to know one thing, Carter. Are you working for Jane Glasglow?"

"Why?" He stalled.

"Just answer the question." I reached over and took his salad plate remembering that he is very allergic to green vegetables; I didn't want him to drop dead before I got my information out of him. He had almost quit breathing one night when he ate dinner with me that Tommy had put green stuff into. I think Tommy did it on purpose but I couldn't prove it.

"Maybe I am, but I can tell you one thing for certain, she's screwing around on her husband with the veterinarian and she is not real fond of you."

"So?"

"So, watch out for her and Al Smith or you may get into something that Mac can't get you out of. By the way I heard you kicked the shit out of the good doctor last night."

All of a sudden there was a hissing sound—followed by a deafening explosion.

Carter jumped up, pulled his gun from his shoulder holster, threw the table over on its side, and shoved me down all in one motion. I was on the floor with Caesar salad mixed with water, coffee and cappuccino all over me. Big man was in his sniper position and aiming at the cappuccino machine.

"Stay down, Jesse, I'll check it out." With that he reached for his ankle holster. You have to admire anyone that ready to kill a cappuccino machine. Maurice came screaming in our direction as I tried to get up.

"Please put your weapons away, sir. It was just a pressure valve stuck on the machine. And you, Madam, and I use that term loosely, are not welcome in here anymore."

I gave him a look and stated, "Carter, shoot him."

Carter was only too happy to comply. He pointed both guns at the little maitre d' from hell and said, "Apologize to the lady now."

Maurice started shaking. "Of course, I was only kidding. Madam, we look forward to your coming in on a daily basis. In fact, we can hardly wait to see you again."

I smiled at him. "And my dog?"

"Of course."

"Okay, Carter, we can sit again." I grabbed a napkin off the floor and mopped dressing off of me. This is the very reason I figure I should wear jeans and a T-shirt. If I had been decked out, my outfit would have been ruined. Now I could just blend it into my jeans.

Maurice was not finished. He motioned another waiter to bring more coffee, tea, and cappuccino.

"Water," Carter said.

"Of course, and water." Maurice snapped his fingers. "Naturally, there will be no charge for the meal."

"I really don't think you need all that caffeine," I admonished Carter.

"It helps me stay on top of things, Jess."

"If you got on top of anything else, we would need bail money. So you're telling me in that oh, so subtle way of yours, that Jane is after me?"

"Only because I care about you. Of course, if you tell anyone, I will be forced to deny it."

"So what were you checking on in records today?" I asked as innocently as possible.

He stopped chewing. "Whatever you do, don't look into the Glasglow's deeds."

"What about the deeds?"

"I am trying to give you a clue woman. For God's sake, take it. I gotta go. Take care of yourself."

"Before you go, what do you know about Anna Hartman and her sister Star?"

"Star's in town? That woman is cold, Jesse. I used to know her years ago. Always seemed jealous of Anna. Her last boyfriend was some English guy with a title. Anna didn't approve. Star didn't care. Turned out he was only after Star for Anna's handouts. He had only a title, no money so Star had to go begging back to Dirth. She has always tried to undermine Anna and get to her money through Dirth. That's about all I can tell you."

It was a start.

I decided to go to the office. Sasha was typing her brains out when I came in. She looked up at me, then at her watch. "How nice of you to come to work today. Love the greasy look too. Been to lunch I see."

"Yes, I have, Sasha. I decided to hell with a fork and just grazed at the salad bar. Who has called and what do they want?"

She thrust a stack of post-it notes at me. They all stick together. I hate that. She knows it.

I sat down at my desk and thought who I should call first. Then the deed thing. Jason, I had to find out what was going on with him. Great time for Tommy to leave.

I decided to harass Jane. I dialed her number. The answering machine picked up. "You may leave a message for the Glasglows."

I announced who I was, what I wanted, and asked if they would be kind enough to call me back. Then I got up out of my chair, threw my duffel over my shoulder, and decided to go to the school to deal with Jason.

Jason's school is very preppy. Luckily, I could afford it and usually he acts responsibly. He had a pretty rough beginning with his mother. I got the feeling he really did want to learn but was still hurt over his mother's leaving him with me. He, therefore, decided to test my boundaries. The kid did not need to be told that his mother was into gambling and drugs. He already knew this by the time I had gone to court and gotten custody. Now I took a deep breath and decided it was time for Tough Love 101.

I walked into the old two story white school with its four white columns. I suppose they were trying to be discreet about being an old money school. I proceeded to the headmaster's office. Mr. Walker used to be a preacher; then his wife had a nervous breakdown and left him to raise their four kids alone. I admired that about him. But that was about all. He was very good-looking about thirty-eight, six-foot and very patronizing. Unable to let go of that preacher thing, he grabbed my hand with both of his—one hand on top of the other.

"Mrs. Statham, so nice of you to drop by."

"Seeing how Jason allegedly tried to burn the school down I thought maybe you might want to talk to me." He motioned me to a purplish velvet high back chair. He closed the stained glass door behind him. Probably reminds him of a pulpit, I thought.

"Oh, that little problem. Yes, I think we should discuss it."

Lord, he was calm.

I pulled my shirt down a little more and asked, "Can you really prove Jason started the fire?"

He smiled at me. "Mrs. Statham, I don't have to prove anything. You see, someone saw your son." He leaned back into his black leather chair folding his hands together to form a steeple.

My turn. "Who saw him?"

"One of our honor students."

"My son, Jason, is also an honor student. I want names. Also, evidence would be nice."

He half rose out of his chair on that one. "I don't see where names would get us anywhere. Suffice it to say Jason has, shall we say, a problem dealing with authority. I now see where that might come from."

Such a sweet man. I leaned back in my chair, crossed my legs, and gave him my most antagonistic look. "Look, Reverend Walker. Oh I forgot you have given that up. I'll just cut to the bottom line. As much money as I shell out to this school, I think that should more than cover a small fire that Jason may or may not have started. As I asked earlier, can you prove it?"

"Mrs. Statham, maybe if Jason had a better authority figure around him, he wouldn't be quite, so shall we say, wild."

I answered back. "He is not, as we shall say, as wild as your son and I have total control of Jason. It seems pretty obvious to me that you are in denial about this son of yours. If I were you, I would consider counseling for your family. Now go get your eyewitness or shut up and drop the charges."

He got off his throne and said, "Let's just consider this little discussion closed for now. Will you please leave?"

"Of course," I said as I reached up to shake his hand, which he withdrew, like I was a snake handler. "If you have anymore problems with Jason just give me a call. It's always a pleasure."

Hurriedly, I walked down the long hallway. When I reached the van, I angrily grabbed the door to get in and felt a ripping white-hot pain sear into my hand. I looked down. Blood was running between my fingers to the ground. I stared at my hand as if it were an alien.

I leaned down to look at the door handle. Someone had glued a razor blade to the underside. I couldn't get in the car. I ran back into the school.

"Mrs. Statham, did we have an accident?" Walker asked with the sensitivity of a crocodile.

I was in pain. I reached into Walker's front pocket with my other hand and grabbed his handkerchief. He tried to pull away but I leaned into him. I wrapped my hand with the handkerchief to stop the bleeding.

"No, I had one. I hope this place is heavily insured."

He reached toward my hand. "Here let me take a look at that. We need to get you to the nurse immediately."

I stepped back holding my arm out of his reach. "I need to use your phone. I can get my own medical treatment." I practically knocked him down on the way to his office to use the phone.

"I'll dial for you," he offered.

"No. Just get the hell out of my way. I will manage." I shut the door on him. I called the paper; its office wasn't far from the school. I put my hand over the headmaster's trashcan to catch the blood.

"Crystal, I'm at the school. I cut my hand on a razor, and I need you to come get me."

"Why? Did you try to slit your wrist without me?"

"Cute. I am not kidding. I hurt like hell and I'm bleeding all over the place. Hurry." Turning to hang the phone up, I knocked half of the papers on Walker's desk to the floor. Damn! I was clumsy. As I bent down to pick them up, I noticed Sentinel Farms on a document. That was the name on the deed at the records department. The paper trail that Dirt, as I had so fondly thought of him, had started. What in the hell was Walker doing with it? I slipped the paper into the pocket of my jeans with my free hand. By now pain was shooting down my injured arm and blood pooled up in the wastebasket that I hung my arm over.

Crystal ran into the office with Walker breathing down her neck. She looked at my bloodied hand, then at me. Blessed blackness.

When I woke up, I was in the emergency room. A very young doctor, a teenager perhaps, was standing over me. Great, I get Doogie Howser, a fourteen-year-old medical prodigy. He looked too happy.

"Good, you are awake. You gave us quite a scare."

"Who are you?" I asked.

"Doctor Young. I know the name fits." He grinned.

"What happened to me? I mean after getting my hand cut I am a little foggy on the rest."

"Must have been something you were allergic to on that razor. I gave you a shot of adrenaline. Are you feeling better?"

"Where's the razor blade?" I demanded, trying to get up. My head was spinning so much that Dr. Young was a blur of black ponytail—good-looking blur at that.

"I don't know. I'll get your friend for you. She is very worried about you. By the way, what are you allergic to?"

"Oh, some chemicals. I'm not really sure unless I come into contact with them. You don't have a clue what knocked me out, do you?"

"No, but you're back now. That's all that really matters. I'll go get your friend. The cuts on your hand were deep, and your hand will be sore for a few days. You didn't need but about five thousand stitches.

Just kidding, try to be careful will you? Your blood sugar is fine and here are some prescriptions." What words of wisdom from one so young.

Crystal was hovering near the door. She held my pocketbook away from her. I forget she's scared of guns.

"I'm taking your butt home," Crystal announced giving me a stern look.

After nurses insisted on rolling me to Crystal's car, I squirmed into her tiny front seat trying to get comfortable. Getting a six-foot frame into a Jaguar isn't easy. Naturally, the car had to be red. It reminded me of my cut hand and the razor blade.

"Take me to the school to get my van, please." I was getting claustrophobic in the small space.

"Jesse, you need to go home. Johnathan can get your van."

"No, I have to check the door out. Someone put a razor blade in the door handle. Did you find it?"

She was taking the curb at a hundred miles an hour gearing down then slapping her foot back down on the accelerator. Then she stomped the clutch as if it were a bug.

"Lt. Cooper is looking into that. I don't know what he found. It was all I could do trying to call an ambulance with Charles Walker chasing me with release papers."

"Did you sign them?"

"No. I threatened to put his ass on the front page of the paper if he didn't shut the hell up; then I called Mac. He said he would find Johnathan. I told him I would get you home and that's what I intend to do."

"Crystal, I want to go to the school. I'm fine. Give me your phone so I can call Johnathan. In fact, I'm hungry. Let's go get some wings and cappuccino." I knew that would get her.

"Damn. All right, stubborn ass." She threw her phone toward me and I called Johnathan with my good hand.

When we got to the van, I unfolded my squashed body from the torture car. I walked to the door and bent down. The razorblade was gone. Now, why didn't that surprise me? I figured Walker had it by now. I checked under the van for a bomb. Didn't see one and got in. Crystal and I headed for the coffeehouse.

Chapter Fourteen

After we had gotten seated at the Brewer's and were munching on Buffalo wings with Ranch dressing, Crystal finally decided to talk to me.

"Jesse, I give the hell up."

"On what? I asked as I hurriedly picked up a buffalo wing before she sucked them all down. I was beginning to twitch from the adrenaline and caffeine.

"Oh, life in general." She sighed loudly as she always did, only now it seemed intensified a hundred times.

"Oh come on, Crystal, things can't be that bad. How do you think I feel having to prove that Jason's not an arsonist."

"But, Jesse, you decided to raise him. I didn't. My children have sense."

"Oh really? One we had to sneak out of a cult, and the other with a slutty looking wife. Yes, I would definitely call that tolerance to the max, Crystal."

"As I said, Jesse, you are the one who decided to bring, not only Jason into your otherwise happy home, but also an ex con by the name of Tommy. By the way, where in the hell is he? I haven't heard you mention him."

"He left on some strange mission last night. Wouldn't say where he's going. Jonathan was very nice about lending him money and all. That struck me as strange. You know Jonathan. He is never nice about money, period."

Crystal scarfed up the last of the buffalo wings while we waited for our veggie melts.

"You mean he's gone? What in the hell are you doing for food?"

"Drop dead. We'll get by just fine. I intend to go by KFC tonight, as a matter of fact. A new change for us will be to have some chicken that hasn't been stir-fried or sautéed. Maybe I'll even go get fish. How's that for living dangerously?"

"Pretty good for you. I didn't think you knew how to eat normal anymore. What's going on with the Glasglows anyway? I mean, are they going to buy up everything in sight by the end of the year?"

"What are you talking about, woman?" I had stopped chewing my veggie melt.

"Just this morning I heard she had made an option on the mortgage of the racetrack. I thought you knew."

"No, I didn't know." Where in the hell is she getting this kind of money?"

"Word has it that she is seeing a preacher on the side."

I hit the underside of the table with my hand. That hurt.

"You mean besides Smith? You mean the woman is having two affairs at one time. I'm sorry, Crystal, but she just does not look that damn good."

"I know, life sucks doesn't it? I mean all I have is midget man going after me and she has two hunks. Go figure." She champed down on the last of the curly fries that had come with her veggie melt.

I sat there trying to go figure. Jane was covering all her bets, but had she also been messing around with Dirt and figured into his death as well? I needed a drink so I ordered white wine to go with the adrenaline. Naturally, Crystal had something to say about this.

"I see we are moving happy hour up to noon."

"Oh shut up. I need to think and I can't possibly do so while you suck on the carcass of a dead chicken and then tell me Jane has possibly three men, not counting her husband, on the side. Damn, Crystal, no one is that good." I drank my wine mulling around the thought.

"What if she killed Hartman?" I blurted out. "Or had him killed? Now there is poor Caroline dead. You know Anna doesn't seem that broken up to me. What if they are all in it together somehow?" My arm was throbbing from the tetanus shot I had gotten at the hospital.

Crystal picked up a Sweet and Low and slapped the poor pink package as though trying to kill it. She began stirring and clanging her spoon on the side until I thought I would have a nervous break down in her coffee mug." She eyed me. "Why would they be in this together? Where is the demon beast today?"

" At home, I got him the cutest little camera…DAMN the camera! Why hadn't I thought of it before? I mean think about the custody battle they are warring over with Classy. What if all that is just a front? Think about it. First, Jane goes after the horse, then the paper. Now, she wants the track. She already has Smith in her pocket. All Anna has to do is bury the son of a bitch. She couldn't stand him anyway. What if they were in on this together? By the way, did I mention I met Smith's son?"

Crystal was staring at me through narrowed eyes. "Where do you come up with this shit?" she asked.

"It is beginning to become very clear now what Smith was doing at the courthouse today."

"What?"

"Hiding evidence," I'll bet.

"What evidence, and what about Barney's camera?"

"Crystal, how can you work for a major newspaper and still not have a clue as to what I am talking about?"

"Excuse the hell out of me for not being as strange as you are. I mean all I see is a woman with money buying a horse, a newspaper, and obviously having a lot of sex on the side."

"Think about what you just said."

She looked up. "Oh, I get the idea now. God, you're good."

I just smiled and thought, yes, I am.

On the way out I telephoned Sasha to find out what was going on at the office.

"Sasha, it's me. What's going on?"

"For one thing you're not here, and I suppose you expect me to do all the work while you get all the glory? Where are you? Mr. Live has been in here three times this morning looking for you."

"I bet that made your heart go pitter patter. I'm on my way to the track to ask some questions. Have I got any messages other than Evil One's?"

"As a matter of fact, Anna Hartman called to ask for an appointment."

"Did you give her one?"

"How could I when I didn't know where you were?"

"Fine, just call her back and tell her I will be back around four. See you later, Sasha." I hung up and turned down the dusty road to the track thinking about the two rednecks that had tried to tango with me at the gas station. That didn't make sense either. I had too many loose ends out there to try and tie up.

I parked the van in my usual place and started toward the office. I walked in and didn't see anyone. Where was Mac? Must be with one of the horses. I hoped Johnathan had told him I was all right. I walked through his office to the walkway where the horses are kept. It was quiet except for the pawing of hooves, swishing of tails, and swatting of occasional horse flies. As I approached Classy's stall, I heard him nicker. I dug a sugar cube out of my pocket.

Then, I noticed the piece of paper I had taken from Walker's office. I leaned against the wall and read it. It was a deed to Sentinel Farms. What was Walker doing with it? I remembered what Carter had said about Glasglow's deeds. But this one was legit. Or was it?

My hand was hurting again and I still had an appointment with Anna. I gave Classy one last sugar cube and started out. He moved forward in the stall. Then it hit me. I had been so busy chasing my tail that I had not given the sweat on Classy a lot of thought. Why had it been on Classy? The only reason I could think of was that good old Dirt had not had time to bathe him. Wonder if Cooper had found out anything about that. I doubted it. Getting back into the van, I headed back toward the office.

The greeting I got when I walked in was surreal. Sasha raced to the door before I could get it open.

"Are you okay? I was so worried about you. After we hung up, Johnathan called me and told me what happened. Why didn't you tell me? Who would do such a thing? Kids are getting out of control. I bet it was Jason."

I stopped the urge to slap her. I finally made it past her to her desk. "What have kids got to do with anything, Sasha?"

"It happened at school. I just figured maybe Jason was mad at you for something."

"Jason did not do this. I can't believe you would think that he did."

"Jesse, he is a little hard to handle. Maybe he's acting out."

"I don't think so. After all, there are several other people who actually don't like me as shocking as that is I'm pretty sure it was one of them. I am going into my office. Get on the phone and tell Ronald asshole that I will see him now."

"He's not going to like having to come down to your office."

"Ask me if I give a damn; then go do it." I slammed the door with my good hand. Reaching into my mini refrigerator with my working hand, I grabbed a Diet Coke. I had to put it between my knees to open it. This is just great, I thought.

I had almost finished the Coke when Ronald Live came waltzing in the door.

"Ms. Statham, I need to talk to you about the way you are single handedly ruining the fine name of Equine Fidelity."

"Try not to hold back, Ronald. Tell me how you really feel."

"Do not get smart with me. I want you to be informed that I put a call in to the Chairman of the Board. I promise he will deal with you. I have a, let's say feeling, that you will not be here very much longer."

"What's his name?" I asked quietly.

Flustered, he responded, "I don't know his name, but I went into great detail with the list I have made about your infractions of company policy."

I crossed the room and was almost standing on top of him.

"Why don't you just admit it, Live? You don't have a clue about who owns this company. I do. I promise to make sure that he or she knows what a great job you do around here sitting on your up tight ass humping anything that gets in front of you. That is if you can reach it. Now, get out. I have an appointment in five minutes. You do know what an appointment is, don't you? That would be where I sit down with real clients who pay premiums that pay your salary. I have to go pee. Why don't you write that in your report?"

I walked to the bathroom. What a shit. He hadn't even noticed my mangled hand, which was beginning to hurt. I grabbed for the bottle of Tylenol in the medicine cabinet then Sasha banged on the bathroom door. "Jesse, your next appointment's here."

I dropped the bottle to the floor. I couldn't get the damn thing open with my bandaged hand. I hate childproof bottles. The only way I could get this damn thing open would be to shoot it open. I opened the door. Sasha saw my predicament and reached down, picked the bottle up, and easily opened it.

"Here are two. Will that be enough? Anna's in my office. Do you want me to show her in?"

"Please," I sighed.

Sasha glanced back. "Are you sure you're all right? I can reschedule her if you want."

"No, I'm fine. Just a little sore. I'll see Anna now." I sat at the desk again.

Anna was wearing another little number today, this one blue. I wondered if she got them from a mail order place. I had never seen anything like these getups at Wal-Mart. She sat in the navy leather chair to my left. Strange, a small smile played across her face. I wondered what was so damn funny. She was looking at my bandaged hand.

"What did you do to your hand, Jesse?"

"An accident. I cut it."

"That's too bad," she clucked. "But I need to go over this policy with you, Jesse. If you have the time."

"Sure. What do you want to know?" I watched her closely as I reached over and clicked the computer to her policy. Her file jumped on to the screen.

"I just wanted to know if the double indemnity clause is in effect."

"That's for the horse, Anna, not Dirth."

"I know. If something happened to Classy, would Equine Fidelity pay double?"

"Has something happened to him?" I leaned back in my chair and stretched.

"No, it's nothing like that. If something did happen though, would it?"

"No, we insure only for the value of the animal at the time of death. Classy is highly insured because he holds so many wins. Mac told me that his studbook is full for the next four seasons. You don't have a thing to worry about. Just keep paying your payments and have F.I. check on him now and then. You should be fine."

"What about Jane Glasglow?"

"Her claim won't stand up in court if she pursues it. Has she been hassling you?"

"Sort of—on an hourly basis. She can go straight to hell as far as I'm concerned. That's all I needed to know, Jesse. I hope you won't sue the school about your hand."

How did she know about the school? I hadn't told anyone where I was when I got hurt. I got up to walk her out and deliberately knocked her handbag over. A small tube of super glue fell out along with a pack of straight edge razor blades.

Anna bent over to retrieve her handbag. She hurriedly crammed the items into it.

"You always carry around razor blades, Anna?' I could feel the blood rushing to my face. It was taking all I had not to tear her throat out.

She took a step back. "Those, I didn't know I still had them. I bought the blades to remove the sticker from my car. Why?"

I grabbed her by the arm and physically shoved her back into the chair.

"Look, you mop-haired, conniving, sniveling bitch. You know exactly what I'm talking about. You have really got to be psychotic to have pulled a stunt like that. Tell me why you did it." I demanded.

Anna came back with "You can't prove anything. Go ahead; call the police. They will just laugh at you."

I said quietly. "Oh no, I won't need the police to deal with you. If you don't start talking, I swear I'll chase your ass till the whole town thinks you are one more paranoid bitch. Think about it."

She put her face into her hands, her lank hair making a veil across it. Her shoulders started shaking.

She sniffed through tears. "I know you're not going to believe me, but I had to put that razor blade on your door."

"You're right. I don't."

She still wouldn't look up. I walked to the desk and slammed my good hand down. She jumped. Good, now I could see her face.

"I had to. I can't tell you why. Go ahead and kill me. You can't possibly hate me as much as I hate myself," she cried.

"I'm pretty sure I could. Who or what has got you jumping through hoops, Anna? I thought that since Dirth died, you actually might get some of your backbone back."

"Call the police, Jesse. If you don't, I'm leaving." She rose from the chair.

"Anna," I called after her. "Let me give you some advice. Watch your ass, because I intend to be on it." She gently closed the door on the way out.

I strode through the door after her and almost mowed down Sasha.

"Sasha, I'm going home. I'll see you tomorrow."

"Do you want me to drive you?"

"I'll be fine, Sasha." I turned back to her. "But thanks for caring."

I drove through the traffic feeling numb, hoping that Johnathan had come up with something for dinner.

When I pulled in the driveway, Barney, Johnathan, and Jason were waiting on me. Johnathan looked at my hand and I saw his lips tighten. He was not happy.

"I'm home." I declared, cheerfully.

Jason grabbed my duffel from the van. Barney sniffed my shoes. I collapsed on the sofa in the den. Barney jumped up and lay down next to me.

"Here, drink this." Johnathan handed me a cup of hot tea. I knew he was upset now. He hated making hot tea. I was so cold. I held the hot cup in my good hand trying to warm it.

"Where did Jason go?" I asked Johnathan.

"Kevin's mother came by to pick him up. He's going to stay the night with them. I figured you could use the rest."

"I'm fine, Johnathan. He didn't have to go over there."

"Are you ready to tell me what happened?"

I took a deep breath and began. "At the school someone put a razorblade in the door of the van."

"Let me see your hand." I held it up to be examined.

"I'm fine. Just a little confused. Anna Hartman did this to me deliberately."

Johnathan frowned. "How do you know?"

"She came by this afternoon and her pocketbook fell open, and out came the blades."

"Why would she do that?" Johnathan persisted.

"I'm not clear on the why, but I am positive that somehow she killed her husband."

"Can you prove it?"

"Not yet, but I will. What's for dinner?" The telephone rang.

"Jesse, it's Carter." There was static on the line. He must be on a cellular phone.

"What's up, Carter?" My hand hurt like hell.

He said, "I heard about the incident today. I wanted to tell you that there is something weird going on at Sentinel Farms. You need to check out the horses there. If you don't get killed first."

"What makes you think I may get killed?" I demanded.

"Something I overheard, gotta go." Click. He had hung up. Great!

Johnathan had made clam chowder. That is the only comfort food I need. I ate three bowls and went upstairs to try to go to sleep. Instead, I tossed and turned. The pills I took for the pain worked for an hour then I hurt as the next three hours crept by. I sat up trying not to wake Johnathan. Barney rose from his pillow.

I motioned to him and we went downstairs to the kitchen. I gave him a cookie. He looked at it and did his stretching act and curled up next to my foot. I reached down and popped the mini cam from his collar and stuck a new roll of film in, tossing the other on the table.

I picked up the cup of chamomile tea I had made and sipped; it was not helping.

Jason had put my bag on the kitchen table, so I leaned over and started sorting through it not really looking for anything in particular—just trying to kill time. I rummaged around in the bag and felt my schedule book. What the hell? I might as well pull it out and look at my schedule for the rest of the week.

I saw that I had three new clients. I was slated to go to their ranches and look at their horses. Maybe one of them would be insurable. Some people could get mad when I told them their horses were not going to get a policy. When I tell people that you cannot insure a preexisting medical problem, they don't understand. To them their horses are perfect, just as mine are to me. That was not necessarily so with the insurance company. There was one case I had where the horses were switched for the veterinarian. Hell, I thought. What was it Carter had said to me about the horses at the college? I needed to go out there. I looked at the clock on the wall. It was three in the morning.

All of a sudden Barney jumped up from the floor and ran for the back door snarling and barking at the same time. I reached into my bag again trying to find my gun. The doorknob slowly turned. By now Barney was going ballistic. I pulled my forty-five from the bag and stood my ground. I saw an umbrella come through the door. Barney grabbed at it ripping it from the hand that held it.

"Mean Dog. Go way."

"Tommy! What in the hell are you doing home?" I put my gun down.

"You hurt. I come home."

"Where were you and how did you find out?"

He walked over to the table and stood by it. "I home now. You be all right."

"That's all you are going to tell me?"

"You need go to bed. That all." He marched off toward his room. Barney had the umbrella in a kill position with his head shaking it vigorously back and forth. I was going to the college, Drake College.

Chapter Fifteen

When Barney and I pulled up, I turned the lights off and grabbed my flashlight. I hadn't leashed Barney since only one of my hands was working.

The Horse Barn at the college is enormous. The animal research center building sits next to it. Something moved across one of the upstairs windows. I stood by the van waiting to see if the shadow came back to the window. It didn't. Things were very quiet outside. Well, I thought, what in the hell do you expect, Jesse; it is four o'clock in the morning? I could have sworn the figure looked like Ken. That was ridiculous, what would he be doing here in the middle of the night?

Barney and I made our way to the front of the barn. God, I was hot, my shirt sticking to me in the humid night air. The barn was made out of red boards in the shape of an old-fashioned barn. There were paddocks with white fencing on three sides. I could smell manure from the tin shed where caretakers had probably stored it from last night's mucking. Cheap labor, I thought. Bring a kid to college here and you could get a lot of work for free. I noticed that the wire around the top of the stalls looked torn. I also noticed the paint was peeling. In fact, the place had gone to hell since I had last seen it.

I was getting hotter, sweat pouring off me. Maybe I had a fever, no a hot flash. My skin was on fire, my scalp burning my hair off. It was drizzling rain. My life is so wonderful.

I called Barney who had been marking the manure pile with his scent and crept into the barn. There were at least fifty stalls on each side of the place. A giant exhaust fan was blowing away in the top, and I could hear horses shifting from side to side, their tails swishing, and soft nickers as I made my way past the student horses to the faculty horses.

These stalls were definitely in better shape. There were bronze nameplates on the doors. I flicked on the flashlight and read Samson's Delight, Touch of Class, Midas Touch. Great names, I thought until I came to the last one. It read Anna's Revenge. I looked in the stall and spotted Classy's double looking back at me. I heard footsteps, flicked off the light and stepped into the stall dragging Barney with me. The horse started snorting. I put my hand on him and rubbed, pleading silently with Barney to be quiet. The footsteps grew closer then stopped in front of the stall. Shit. I couldn't see out.

"We have to take him tonight," Jane Glasglow spoke.

"I don't think that's very smart, Jane. The racetrack will be empty tomorrow night too," a male voice answered.

Al Smith. What was that son of a bitch up to?

"No, it has to be tonight. I will not have that insurance veterinarian screw up anything else. He's already suspicious now. So when he comes for the pre-race check up, he'll have his precious Classy back. Besides, Anna is getting harder to control."

I heard the latch turning. Oh God. I had left my bag in the car. They must have seen the van when they got here.

"Did you hook the trailer lights up, Al?"

"Damn, I forgot," he said, closing the latch again.

"Go do it; we don't want the police pulling us over for that. You are so stupid sometimes. Why do I put up with it?"

Al whispered, "Baby, you know why you put up with it, want me to remind you?"

Oh my God, were they going to copulate here? In front of Barney? Gag a maggot. I prayed the man would be a premature ejaculator.

He evidently was, and I tried not to vomit and figured I would go deaf now that I had heard this hideous act. On the other hand if Crystal were here, she would have probably joined in.

I listened and rubbed the horse until I could no longer hear mating moans on the walkway. I felt an overwhelming need for a cigarette. I looked for Barney, but he had curled up in the corner on some bedding and was asleep. I unlatched the door and motioned for Barney, then climbed on Classy. I was bareback and leaning down hanging on to his mane for balance. I guided him with my legs; Barney followed.

We softly walked down the walkway to the opening and I saw two figures bent over the back of a truck. I would not let that bitch get Classy.

I could hear yelling when I started for the wooded area that went over to Anna's place.

I couldn't go there. She had already tried to amputate me. I didn't feel she would offer refuge. I might as well ride him home. I could cut across the woods and go through a couple of subdivisions. Classy seemed happy enough. We walked slowly in the rain as I talked to the horse. Barney scouted. My hand was bleeding through the gauze. Somehow I had ripped my stitches open. There was no way to avoid going through Vernon's yard and as we tiptoed across it, Classy took a moment to relieve himself of his dinner. What a good horse.

Things were starting to come together in my mind, what little I had left. First, Anna has the horse. No. Dirth has the horse. Okay then he dies and Jane buys it, then Anna gets Classy back.

Classy suddenly sneezed and I almost toppled off. I regained my balance placing both hands on his warm shoulders.

Where was I? Oh yeah, then from Dirth to Jane to Anna. Now Dirth is dead, so is Caroline. Why? What did they have in common? F.I. the bastard was a killer! No, that didn't make sense. Okay, F.I. insured Classy and Caroline worked for F. I.

Hold that thought I told myself as we cut across the lit streets of a nice subdivision. Classy took that moment to try and graze on an azalea bush out of someone's yard before I could do anything about it. Classy had pulled it up by the roots. Barney was deliberately going up to fenced in yards and antagonizing the dogs there. They began raising hell. I urged Classy on with my legs reaching down to pull the azalea bush from his mouth. We continued our walk.

Then Smith and Jane, Smith must have meet Caroline somehow and become involved. Hmmm. Not sure. Jesse think. Jane hates Anna. Anna hates Smith. Smith screwing Jane, Dirth dead, Caroline screwing Smith? What about Star? She couldn't be that damn innocent if everyone else was guilty. The pictures needed developing that Barney had around his neck.

God I was tired as we made our way onto our property.

I finally saw my house ahead. As Barney trotted to the barn, Classy and I followed. I saw Johnathan, standing in the morning drizzle, shaking his head.

"Jesse, what in the hell are you doing and how much is this going to cost?"

"I stole a horse. Will you and Tommy go and get my van? I left it at Drake College in front of the big barn. Oh, I couldn't sleep. But I love you."

I put Classy in Prince's stall then locked the barn and walked over to my little office, and picked up the twelve-gauge I keep there then proceeded to the desk where I took out shells and loaded it. Then I went to the phone and called Mac. He answered on the second ring. Normally he answers on the first ring. Must have been in a coma.

"Mac, something is about to happen out here. I think you need to get over here. Can you bring F.I. too?"

"Jesse, have you lost your mind? It's barely daylight. What's so important?"

"I have Classy."

There was a pause. "You what?"

"You heard me. Wake up. I have the real Classy and he goes by the name of Anna's Revenge."

I made coffee while I waited. I was getting very tired by the time Mac and F.I. arrived. Johnathan and Tommy appeared behind them. Tommy said he would make breakfast.

I told a very sleepy F.I. what I wanted him to do. He looked at me strangely but nodded. F.I. followed me into the office. I had laid out the autopsy on Dirth and the blood test he had taken on Classy the day Classy had been tubed for colic—the day before Dirth had died.

"Well," I said.

F.I. reached into his pocket and pulled out his reading glasses. He bent over and examined the two documents.

"That's not normal."

"What?" I asked.

"You see where the test for drugs currently in the system is?" He pointed with his finger to Classy's blood test. "There are traces here of Paronyl. Shouldn't have shown up there."

"Why not?" I was almost on top of him now.

"There is no way Classy was on that drug. It's a tranquilizer and I didn't prescribe one for him. So look at the blood test on Dirth; it's also marked with the same drug."

"Are you telling me that someone gave it to Dirth?"

He scratched his head. "They wouldn't have to. It has a strange way about it. If Dirth's heart problem was bad enough, hell the fumes from the horse's sweat could do it."

"Shit, F.I., why didn't you see this before?"

"What in the hell would I be doing with Dirth's autopsy, Jesse?"

He was right. I was just tired and hurting so I decided to blame him.

He patted my arm. "That girl had a big crush on someone and I believe it got her killed. A damn shame."

I looked at F.I. "Suppose she had this crush on let's say a veterinarian. Then she helped this veterinarian switch medicine reports on another veterinarian?"

He slowly nodded at me in understanding and left.

I asked Mac to help me load Classy, so that we could bring the real Classy to the track.

Chapter Sixteen

After delivering the horse to the track, I spent the rest of the morning on the phone. First, I called J. P. and asked her to meet me at Drake College in thirty minutes. I also phoned Ken. There was no answer so I paged in 666 so he would be sure to get the message. Finally, I called Ms. Helpful in tax records. She informed me that the college was three years behind in its property taxes and that a Sentinel Farms was in the process of foreclosing on the school.

Tommy had taken Barney's film to be developed and was back smiling as he handed me the white packet of pictures.

I whistled as I studied them. One shot of Johnathan's crotch, another of Tommy's. I smiled thinking of what fun I could have with that one. More land shots, Classy's stall shots, Dirth dead shots. A shot of Smith, another of the wall in the stall. Wait a damn minute Smith was in the barn with me when Dirth had been killed? I kept flipping through the pictures what I found was amazing.

This left me with one more question. How in the hell had Dirth gotten into the Paronyl?

I showered and threw on some jeans and a T-shirt. This one announced, "I'm Dressed, What More Do You Want?" Seemed appropriate. Then I drove to the college, an ever-faithful Barney beside me.

As I pulled up, I could see J. P.'s white Cadillac parked out front.

Barney and I were making our way to the front of the barn when again I detected a shadow crossing the window of the upper floor. Just as I had the last time I visited, I ducked into the manure shed and drew my gun out of the back of my jeans where I had put it. I had also put a two and a half-inch steel throwing star, a spur shaped, sharp edged weapon usually used by men, in the nylon ankle holster Tommy had made me for my birthday. I have three such weapons.

I duck walked with the gun up against my chest and made it to the back door of the barn. I could feel Barney's hot breath on my neck. At least I hoped it was Barney. There was a crack between the door jam and I peered through.

Al Smith was leaning against a stall door in conversation with Ben and Jane. Smith was in jeans and a blue denim shirt, seemingly at ease. Jane, not at ease, stood guard in front of the fake Classy's empty stall. What in the hell was she guarding?

In the farthest corner of the room, I could see J. P. tied to a post, her mouth gagged and taped and wished I had brought a camera.

I put a hand on Barney who remained quiet and tried to ease the door open. All heads turned to the door, which sounded like the Hindenburg blowing up. So much for sneaking up. I stood up and trained the gun on Smith as Barney now softly growling and I walked into the barn.

I spoke first. "Guess what I found out last night?"

Six eyes turned and stabbed me. Jane broke the momentary silence. " Please do tell us what you found. Also explain to me why you're not in jail for stealing my horse. Ben, I want her arrested."

The lord of the liquor bottle spoke, "Young woman, you are the cause of this impromptu event, so tell us why you're here."

J. P. was kicking the post with her heels, her face red. Sweat poured off her as she struggled. She was not a happy boss. Maybe she need anger management classes.

I looked directly Jane, "Have you seen my boss?"

Out of the corner of my eye, I could see Smith slowly inching up behind me. So they were going to circle me.

I turned toward Smith with the gun and asked, "Ben, are you really as stupid as you act or are you stupid for real? Because your wife and one of her lovers are going to do away with you in just a matter of time."

Jane jerked her head toward Smith. "Shoot her!"

I sidestepped into Jane and pulled her between Smith, and me; he had now pulled out a nine-millimeter Ruger. I have always wanted one but Johnathan always says, "No, they are too expensive." The Ruger was pointed at Jane now.

Smith bargained. "Look, Statham, we can swap. Your boss for Jane and me getting out of here with the horse."

Out of the corner of my eye, I watched as Barney chewed the ropes off of J. P.'s hands. I had to keep these people focused on me.

"Smith, maybe you're right, but I kind of have a problem with trust. I think it's a childhood issue as I haven't quite resolved it; however, I am in art therapy now so maybe I can trust you oh let's say when hell freezes over. By the way, Jane, how in the world did you have time to have sex with three lovers? I am impressed as is Crystal and half the town."

I had a tight hold on Jane. My arm was tightly wrapped around her throat as I walked backwards. J. P. was now loose and looking pretty pissed. I watched her pick up a pitchfork that was leaning against a post and she and Barney advanced toward Ben.

Jane was now digging her dagger nails into my arms as I tried to hold her. I pressed her throat a little tighter.

"Smith, drop the gun or I will shoot you. Jane, knock it off or I will choke you."

Jane screamed a war cry as J. P. stuck the pitchfork into Ben Glasglow's back knocking him to the ground.

Jane was ripping my arm to shreds as I tried to hold her. She finally managed to knock the gun out of my hand, and I saw J. P. scurry toward it.

Jane wrestled free of me and I slapped the shit out of her and knocked her into a pile of horse manure.

Barney lunged for Smith's arm because he was now pointing the gun toward J. P. and me. Smith fired just missing my head.

I dove into Smith bringing him down under me. We wrestled and he punched me in the face. I kicked at his balls missing, I assume, as he kept punching. Barney savagely was biting him at the same time. J. P. had retrieved my gun and was fiercely pointing it at Smith, "Move one inch, you son of a bitch, and you will die."

Stealthily Jane sneaked up behind J. P. with another gun. Damn, had there been a gun sale I had not known about?

By this time I had Smith by one arm and was trying to get him off me. "J. P., the bitch is behind you uh with a gun of her own."

J. P. turned as if she played for the Harlem GlobeTrotters and smashed Jane in the head with my forty-five. She would need stitches, hopefully even plastic surgery.

While I held Smith, he grabbed me by the throat and was trying to screw my head on backwards. I rammed my finger into his right eye, then shoved his nose toward the back of his brain with the bottom of my hand. His blood pouring, he still fought. As he did, he was trying to push my carotid artery through to the other side of my neck. I knew for sure that the man really wanted to rearrange my anatomy. Maybe he didn't like my looks. Because my hands were slippery with his blood, I was seeing double then the light that Sasha had talked about in her episode at the pool. With a last spurt of energy, I pulled the steel star from my ankle and slashed Smith across the throat.

An hour later J.P., Barney and I found ourselves at the police station again. Only this time Al Smith was in the hospital. Mac, Jane, and Ben bandaged up were sitting next to Ronald Live, Sasha, Star, F.I., along with Johnathan and Ken and Anna. Cooper looked glum. I didn't blame him.

Cooper cleared his throat. "Jesse, I mean, Statham, please go over the incident again, slowly this time."

I had blood all over my clothes and hands, I was sure Sasha disapproved of my latest fashion statement.

"It all started with a woman who had taken all the abuse she could. This person found out that her younger sister was having an affair with her husband. She was scared of him but wanted him to pay dearly for that abuse. The sister also was jealous of her money, so she figured if she could get the husband, she would get the money."

Jane interrupted, "That's what made you steal my horse? Oh, come on."

"It gets better. A lawyer's wife decides to fool around with the husband, too. Only problem is she wants a particular horse he owns. So she gets her other lover to help her obtain the horse. How she kept up sexually is beyond me."

"Lady, you are going to get sued so fast it will make your head spin. Do the words slander mean anything?" Jane fumed.

I waited until she ran out of breath.

"As I was saying, the wife knew the horse better than the husband did. She knew how he loved to boast about Classy's wins. She also knew the horse was sterile. You see she was an expert rider. He didn't know shit about a horse. She couldn't get him to love her, but she could convince him to buy a champion; he had already gotten bored with his baseball team. He loved winning and she knew it. Only she hadn't planned on him selling her horse. That's when she got mad and took a lover, one that was a veterinarian. Right, Ken?"

All eyes turned to F.I. "Don't look at me. I don't have time to have sex."

Ken continued to smile the corners of his eyes not moving.

I went on. "No-not you. Someone who already had a record. Al Smith."

Ben Glasglow shifted uncomfortably. "You can't prove any of this."

At that time Ronald Live decided to chime in. "Ms. Statham, I want you to quit whatever you're doing right now. I will not have you badger my clients in this fashion. People, I am so sorry about this. I will see that she is fired, of course." He turned toward Jane.

Johnathan stood quietly next to Mac and softly advised, "She will speak and you will not have her fired, Live."

"Do I know you? That voice sounds so familiar." Live inquired.

"I am Johnathan, Jesse's husband. Shut up and let her talk."

Ronald reached for his tie and straightened it. "And you would be?"

"I am married to your worst nightmare."

J. P. rolled her eyes and ordered, sarcasm dripping. "Live, shut up or I will have YOU fired."

I continued, "Anna got scared when her husband sold Classy. He would find out through tests that are required by the insurance company that the horse could never produce. That was something Dirth would never forgive—a sterile winner. He would be laughed off the racetrack. Her lover, the veterinarian Al Smith, decided that he would help her and make money at the same time. He was going to switch horses for her. Bring in a ringer. But then he decided to go for broke. He knew Dirth had a heart condition and that if he injected the horse with Paronyl and if he could get Dirth in the stall after Classy had worked out, that the sweat from the horse would kill him." I shut up.

"That is ridiculous," Jane said.

"No, it's not." Not if you knew, and you did, that the fumes from the horse on Paronyl would kill a person with a heart condition," I snorted.

"You can't prove anything," Anna blurted out.

"Yes, I can. Also, Jane stumbled across the fact that there was a lot of money to be made off the foreclosure of Drake College. The place had gone to seed and her preacher friend was trying to get it for their phony company. Sentinel Farms. Seems she promised him a tidy sum. She was running around town buying horses and newspapers with money from her husband's bank account. She handled all his paperwork and finances. He didn't have a clue."

"This is so ridiculous. You can never make this stick." By now Jane was looking haggard.

"Not only can I make it stick, I'll actually enjoy doing so. I have photos." I held up a picture.

Anna cracked. "That's why I had to hurt you, Jesse. Jane said if I didn't, she wouldn't sell Classy back to me and she would shut down the college. I went to school there. The only good times I had were at Drake," she sobbed softly.

Ken stepped forward. "I can prove everything you've done, Jane, including killing Caroline so that she would never be able to rat about swapping the horse records."

"How? I don't even know you." Jane declared.

Ken said. "I know you. I have been following you everywhere for weeks. The people I work for have been very interested to know why you were at the college so much, right next to the animal research center. You knew that Smith was planning on making a comeback selling animals to laboratories again, and so you cooperated with him."

I jumped in. "Ken who in the hell do you work for?"

Ken said "Jesse, I work for the animal protection league. I thought you knew."

Cooper added, "And the DEA, the FBI, firearms and tobacco ect."

"You little shit, you lying little shit." I yelled.

Cooper interrupted again. "That's enough."

"Cooper, I'm not finished yet," I argued.

"Yes, you are. These people are entitled to a lawyer."

I was not giving up that easy. "They have one—Ben Glasglow. Besides, I also want them charged with fraud." Looking straight at Jane and Ben, I accused, "Trying to pass off the other horse for Classy when F.I. examined him. Remember when Jane bought Classy. That's fraud. She also endangered the animal's life with the injection." Then I blurted, "Wait, We need to arrest the head master of the school, too. God, everyone was screwing everyone."

F.I. glared at me. "I repeat; I wasn't."

Chapter Seventeen

We were sitting at home, Johnathan in his chair, I on the couch. Jason sat on the floor.

"How did you figure all this out, Dolls?"

"Well, Paronyl is an animal tranquilizer. It didn't make any sense for it to be in Dirth's body. There were no puncture wounds, so I had to figure out how it had gotten into him."

"Okay, but how could you be so certain as to the Sentinel Farms deal," Johnathan asked.

"Paper trail. It didn't fit at first until I rode Classy home and had to cut across Anna's property. Then I remembered how she had gone to school there. It all started coming together."

"Do you think Anna knew Al was going to kill Dirth?"

"I am not sure that's Coopers problem. I gave the man my photos for God's sake. Yeah, with Cooper hanging in the case like a pit bull to prove it, but I don't know if they can tie Anna into anything. However, now it's the DA's problem. Equine Fidelity is in the clear and Smith is going to live and do time again."

Johnathan asked. "What was in the picture you held up and then turned toward yourself?"

Tommy's crotch shot." I started laughing then howling slapping my arm against Johnathan until he cracked up laughing and Barney howling.

Tommy burst into the room and shouted, "Dinner."

The End

About the Author

Jeannie Sutton Hogue lives in Georgia with her husband and two dogs and cats. She was a horse trainer for twenty years and past president of Georgia's largest writing group. She has written humorous and serious articles which have appeared in horse magazines. She is currently in the process of becoming a licensed private investigator.

Joy Hilliard Padgett teacher, writer, past president and board member of a large Georgia writing group, occasional columnist for the Carroll Star News, and one-time editor of a local newsletter is currently president of the West Georgia Writers Guild, Inc. She and her college professor, songwriting husband of thirty-eight years share three children and six grandchildren and live near Atlanta.